I0568108

THE AUCTION

Lyn Austin

Copyright 2015 Lyn Austin

ANOTHER CHANCE

The horse followed a narrow trail that spiraled up the mountain. Spotlights had been strategically placed in the snow, lighting the path without detracting from the magical ambience. The trail grew ever steeper, and suddenly they were in a small clearing. Michael pulled back the reins, and Ginger immediately came to a halt.

Kat gasped. "Oh, my God, Michael. It's incredible."

The view honestly took her breath away. The moon was almost full, and it had risen to light the gray night with the help of a million stars. White mountains piggybacked each other, ridge after ridge. In the dimness Kat could barely make out the outline of clumps of trees. She felt special yet utterly insignificant at the same time.

Michael put his arms around her and pulled her near. She could smell the musky, clean scent of him, and she was surprisingly warm and comfortable. Despite the past two years, it felt…right.

THE AUCTION

Lyn Austin

www.BOROUGHSPUBLISHINGGROUP.com

PUBLISHER'S NOTE: This is a work of fiction. Names, characters, places and incidents either are the product of the author's imagination or are used fictitiously. Any resemblance to actual events, locales, business establishments or persons, living or dead, is coincidental. Boroughs Publishing Group does not have any control over and does not assume responsibility for author or third-party websites, blogs or critiques or their content.

THE AUCTION
Copyright © 2015 Lyn Austin

All rights reserved. Unless specifically noted, no part of this publication may be reproduced, scanned, stored in a retrieval system or transmitted in any form or by any means, electronic, mechanical, photocopying, recording, or otherwise, known or hereinafter invented, without the express written permission of Boroughs Publishing Group. The scanning, uploading and distribution of this book via the Internet or by any other means without the permission of Boroughs Publishing Group is illegal and punishable by law. Participation in the piracy of copyrighted materials violates the author's rights.

ISBN 978-1-942886-59-4

To Butch, for teaching me to believe in myself.
With you in my life, nothing is impossible.

Acknowledgments

My warmest thanks to Chris Keeslar and the staff at Boroughs Publishing Group. I have never had an editor like Chris, who has given me so much time and expertise to make my writing better than it's ever been. I'm forever in your debt.

Contents

Chapter One

It's amazing what kind of knowledge a girl can glean in a bathroom.

Kat pretended to be intent on fixing a stray lock of hair, while out of the corner of her eye she recognized two snow bunnies of the type that often hung around the local ski resorts of Park City, Utah. A blonde with big hair and a bubbled cleavage leaned toward the mirror and brushed an imaginary speck from her cheek. She spread a new coat of cherry-colored lipstick on her pouting lower lip then checked her sparkling veneers once before turning to her friend. "I swear, Patti, I'm not leaving here tonight without Michael Blake attached to my side."

"How much money did you bring to bid on him?" Patti was gazing at her friend's reflection in the wall-length mirrors and trying without success to make her chest stick out and up as provocatively. She looked like Midge compared to Barbie.

"I could only come up with a thousand, and I had to borrow the last hundred from Tony. I know that's not very much, but I'm hoping that the rest of the hooty women from around here are all friends of his ex and won't dare bid on him. I hear she's such a bitch."

"Are you serious, you borrowed money from your boyfriend to bid on another man for a week? God, Heather, that's even tacky for you."

Heather pulled at the hem of her skin-tight dress, leaving even more of her augmented bust exposed. "If everything goes the way I've got it planned, Michael Blake will be mine soon and Tony will be history."

Patti stared at her companion through the long expanse of mirrors. When she noticed Kat at the other end of the row of polished sinks, Katherine applied fresh lipstick with a feigned disinterest, not wishing to be caught eavesdropping.

The redhead turned back to her friend. "Michael Blake doesn't even know you. How do you know you're his type?"

"Watch and learn, honey. Believe me, I'm his type. I'm every man's type. And by next weekend he'll know me very well. Even if I do have to buy him to get his attention."

"I think you're dreaming. Michael Blake is going to be auctioned off for a lot more than a thousand dollars. He's incredibly gorgeous and generous too, apart from being extremely successf…"

Their voices faded as the door swung closed behind the pair. Kat stood staring at her reflection. Her expression changed from disdain to a renewed determination. Snapping the clasp on her satin evening bag, she whispered to herself, "Your friend's right, Ms. Snow Bunny, Michael isn't going home with you or anyone like you."

She couldn't say what he had intended when he'd accepted an invitation to be one of Park City's most eligible bachelors in Make-A-Wish's New Year's Day local celebrity auction, but tonight Michael Blake would be going home with *her*. Steeling her nerves, she finished up and left the bathroom.

"There you are, Kat, I was just coming to look for you," Georgi scolded gently as Katherine returned to the main room. She was ever the mothering type. "Hurry and sit down. They're about to start."

Taking her seat brought relief to Kat's shaking knees, but the strong resolution she'd felt a few moments before seemed to leave as she stared up at the stage from their front row table.

"I was afraid you changed your mind and ran for it," Georgi said, "but Tara reminded me you always head for the bathroom when you get the jitters."

Tara leaned forward and touched Kat's hand. "There's still time to back out of this. I don't think it's a good idea. There's just got to be a better and easier way."

Her friend's concern touched Katherine and shook her resolve further.

"Lighten up, Tara," Georgi scolded. "Kat can do this. We're here to help you through it; just keep your mind on the final outcome. Remember what the doctor told you."

"Yes. My endometriosis."

"Exactly. Your chances are getting slimmer and slimmer. You're running out of time. Consider this your first sacrifice for the life you're ready to create. You're out on the limb now."

"Yeah," Kat muttered. "So far out, I can't get down."

"Georgi, you seem to have forgotten that Michael is not Kat's husband anymore. The divorce was final almost two years ago. Did you two ever stop to think that maybe he doesn't want to be a daddy?"

"He kept telling me he wanted a family," Kat said sullenly, "but work always came first. He was never home long enough to even try to start one, let alone to raise one."

The surrounding crowd grew louder as the alcohol flowed, so Tara leaned in close. "Kat, someone needs to be the voice of reason for a minute. Michael was in the process of building a huge ski resort, that's true, and I know you took second or maybe even third place lots of times, but I also know he felt the sacrifice was for both of you. And don't forget you were extremely busy with your shop."

"Okay, I'll give you that. I did spend much of my time at the shop and on antique-buying trips," Katherine admitted, "but I was always there for his big important events. Hell, he didn't even make it to my grand opening. I was so embarrassed, what with everybody asking over and over again where he was. I couldn't even tell them, because I didn't know!"

Georgi gave the comment a flick of her hand. "Oh God, Kat, we've heard this all a billion times. And we're not saying you were wrong, but just remember—after that night you started skipping out on Michael's important events too. Revenge is a nasty business. Still, it's all in the past. What's done is done. We've got our eyes on the prize."

Tara shuddered. "I can still see him at the opening of Eagle's Nest, watching and waiting for you, telling the TV news people to wait just a few more minutes because he wanted his wife to help him cut the ribbon. You never showed up."

Katherine ducked her chin and buried her face in her hand. It hadn't been one of her finer moments.

"Let's get out of here," Tara said, grabbing her purse. "Before you regret yet another unfortunate moment."

"There's still time," Georgi admitted in a whisper. The opening music had begun. "You can still back out. On the other hand, this is the best way to make your dream come true. You've told us a hundred times that Michael's DNA would make the perfect baby. Don't give up just shy of the finish line. You may not get another chance. We did our homework on him, too. He's not in any kind of relationship...unless you count his resort as his mistress. Huh. That was kind of the problem in the first place, wasn't it?"

Tara sighed and nodded, putting her hand in Kat's. "Whatever you decide. We're with you."

Katherine's resolve strengthened. The music swelled, promising a dramatic and exciting evening, and she smiled at her friends and gulped a great amount of air into her lungs. She reached out and gave each of their hands a quick squeeze. "Let's make this happen."

Spotlights brightened the stage and crisscrossed the runway as the introductory music and applause receded. Carol Young, a popular local news anchorwoman, dressed in a full-length black sheath, stepped to the podium.

"Good evening, and welcome to our annual Make-A-Wish Foundation local celebrity bachelor auction."

Another round of applause helped cover Kat clearing her throat. She looked to each of her friends to see if they too had suddenly realized the irony of the fundraiser's name in regards to the plan, making wishes come true, but their attention was on the host, so she turned back to the stage.

"We have a wonderful group of bachelors this year, and we want to thank each one for selflessly offering his time. We realize that a week is a long time to be away from a business, and we hope that the women with the highest bids will keep that in mind. Don't keep them *too* busy, girls. We want them to go back to work well-rested…well, maybe not well-rested, but back to work, anyway."

Laughter and more light applause filtered through the banquet room, and the clinking of wine glasses rang in the air. Kat felt the urge for some liquid confidence herself, and she drained her Chardonnay in two gulps.

"Ladies, let's meet our bachelors!"

The hoots, howls, and whistle calls were anything but ladylike. The room's occupants suddenly sounded more like bikers at a strip club. Over the roar, the emcee leaned into her microphone and introduced each man who walked up on stage. Kat barely glanced at the tuxedo-clad lineup, but she did notice that, although Michael was on the far side of the stage, he was the only one wearing a suit instead of a tux. He never was one to conform. Trust him to be the odd man out. She purposely didn't look at him again.

"We thought we'd let you get a quick peek at all six men before we begin. They clean up pretty good, don't they?" Another round of cheering erupted, and Ms. Young raised her elegant arm to quiet everyone. "In your program you will find a detailed description of each bachelor and his statistics. Well, let's say *some* of his statistics. The rest will be revealed to you at the bachelor's discretion."

Her wry wit was a side the audience had never seen of Carol Young on her news program. She was brilliant at winning the women to her side, all while warming them up to part with their cash. Kat admired her even more. She even considered inviting Carol to lunch someday when she was down the mountain in Salt Lake. Carol's afternoon talk show often spotlighted local businesses, so maybe she'd be interested in covering an antiques shop.

"As you know, our men are celebrities from all walks of life, and we hope that their natural talents will be useful to some of you this coming week…though they're surely skilled in more than they say. Still, we can only promise what they offered in their contracts. The rules and regulations are included in the back of your programs, so be sure to check those out before you drop six weeks' paycheck on a hunk—unless you're one hell of a sweet-talker. Then, spend away! It's for a good cause! So, let's meet our first bachelor."

Five of the men walked offstage, and Michael was the first of these. The remaining man—or *boy,* for that's what he looked like to Kat—strutted down the runway.

"Terry Adams is our first bachelor. He lives in Salt Lake City when he's not in New York or L.A. pursuing a successful modeling career."

Georgi leaned into the middle of the table, and Kat and Tara waited. The three had been friends for so long that the look on her face was enough to make them grin in anticipation. She did not disappoint. "Our little Terry looks like he'd be more comfortable at a Ricky Martin concert."

It seemed that Georgi had company in thinking Terry might very well be gay. The bidding started at one hundred dollars, and the following offers came a little sluggishly. They picked up, though, and finally the proceedings closed at fifteen hundred. The winning bidder was a fiftyish woman wearing a stunning red suit. She had diamond studs the size of dimes in her ears, and a frozen face with enough Botox in the chin and cheeks to pay for a villa in the south of France.

"Maybe she's buying her son a late Christmas gift," Georgi offered as the night's intermediary entertainment, a band called The Last Resort, came on stage.

Katherine tried to laugh, but her nerves had returned with a vengeance. Half of Kat wanted Michael to be second so she could get this over and done with, but the other half wanted to put it off as long as possible.

It seemed the men would return to the runway in the order they had stood on the stage, so Michael would be last. It took well over three hours to introduce the other four bachelors, what with the breaks for The Last Resort. Kat did not get up to dance, and she even ducked down and tried to stay out of sight. A sexy but shy rancher raised two thousand dollars. A divorce attorney went to a former client of his, both of whom Kat knew because she too had used the lawyer's services. Next out was a rock-star-looking bad-boy Olympic medalist in downhill racing, and the fifth man was a movie producer and director currently showcasing at the Sundance Film Festival.

The host for the evening took the mic once again. "Ladies, for those of you who were outbid or have been holding on to your purse, now is the time to let it all go. Please, help me welcome to the stage our last bachelor for this year's event, the owner and operator of the prestigious Eagle's Nest Ski Resort here in Park City. I might add that he is well known for his generous support to the Make-A-Wish Foundation and many others organizations as well. Ladies, please welcome…Mr. Michael Blake!"

Though it had been several hours, Michael looked as fresh as when he'd first appeared onstage. He walked casually up the runway and stood with one hand in the pocket of a classic, rich, cloudy gray Armani suit. Kat wondered who had been doing his shopping for him. She hadn't seen him out of ski or work clothes for years. His dark blond hair had been professionally trimmed, which she'd never been able to get him to take the time to do, and she swore he'd had his teeth whitened.

Kat was staring up at him, trying to figure out if indeed his teeth were whiter or if the light was just reflecting off them, when she heard a gasp slip from both of her friends. She quickly looked over and then followed their gazes back to Michael. His lopsided grin and easy-going stance were changing visibly, for he stood transfixed, staring at Tara, clearly just recognizing her. Slowly that glacial stare shifted to Georgi and finally came to rest on Katherine. His smile disappeared, and Kat was close enough to see the old familiar twitch begin to churn in his left cheek. That happened every time he got upset, and the harder it pulsed the angrier he was. From the look of that cheek, he was furious. But if he was pissed at her now, Kat wondered what his reaction would be by the end of the evening.

No one but Michael and the three women seemed to notice anything out of the ordinary; the crowd was still roaring and the music segued into Robert Palmer's "Simply Irresistible." Michael regained his composure, offered the audience his gorgeous smile and moved toward the top-center of the stage.

Georgi sighed. "I guess the phrase 'if looks could kill' would be relevant about now? And an understatement."

"He looks incredible," Tara whispered. "He gets better with age. He looks hotter now than he did when you first brought him back to our apartment. I think we were all a little in love with him, but he only had eyes for you, Kat. It was always you."

"Well, remember two years ago?" Katherine snapped. "I wasn't a priority in his life then. No other woman was involved, maybe, but how would you like being replaced by bulldozers, blueprints, ski lifts, restaurants and fundraisers? Things change. People change. After six months of counseling sessions—that I mainly attended myself—I got the picture. He just doesn't feel the same anymore. You both saw the way he just looked at me. He despises me…and I'm finally over him, too. You both know that."

Her two friends looked skeptical.

Georgi shivered and wrapped her shawl around her bare shoulders. "Did you see the way he looked at us? I'm glad he isn't packing heat!"

"Michael's a bit upset, but he'll just have to get over it." Katherine wished she felt as flip as she sounded, but she'd fought to keep her words light. "Have you ever seen a divorce more civil than ours? We gave each other everything and then simply moved on like any civilized couple should do when they've outgrown each other."

"That was the trouble in my marriage," muttered Tara, resting her chin in her hand. "One of us never grew up."

"Aren't you forgetting something, Kat?" Georgi asked. "You do need Michael for one more little thing. That's why we're here, remember?"

They all laughed, albeit nervously.

"You're right, Georgi." Kat looked down at an imaginary watch on her wrist. "And this auction couldn't have come at a better time. According to my biological clock, this week is the perfect time to begin my little project."

She was thirty-five years old, and she knew what she wanted more than anything else. Right now, she wanted a child. Michael's. And while it had taken her awhile to figure out how to obtain her objective, nothing would stop her until she succeeded.

It was the bubble-busted blonde from the ladies' restroom who began the bidding, giving the entry-level bid of one hundred dollars. Michael walked to the edge of the runway once more, never allowing his gaze to veer in the direction of Kat's table. Kat settled into her chair and watched with mild fascination as the bidding bounced from one woman to the next. Things moved quickly but in small increments from twenty-five to fifty dollars. Kat had no intention of bidding on Michael until it was almost over.

"The bids are pretty low," Tara whispered. "What's going on?"

"Tickles me to death," piped up Georgi. "I guess these girls spent their money on augmentations—maybe to keep him after the week is over."

"Michael keeps eyeing that little blonde over there with the enormous ones," Tara commented. "Gold lamé. How chic."

Kat glanced at the woman in question—the bimbo from the bathroom. Heather. She shrugged and turned back to the stage. Heather only had one thousand dollars. She could beat that.

Georgi turned. "There are six women oozing hormones all over your ex, Kat, and you're as cool as Fairbanks in January. No more jealousy?"

Katherine felt her stomach twist. No, she wasn't jealous. She didn't want Michael back in her life except for one, maybe two specific purposes. When those two things had been taken care of, she would sell her house in Park City and start a new life somewhere far away, somewhere Michael would never have to be bothered with her again.

"I told you," she said. "I'm *over* him. That should make things much less complicated in the next few days—and for the rest of my life."

Ms. Young's voice slowed. "Going once…"

Kat realized that while they were chatting the bid had crept up to an astounding three thousand dollars. She noticed the rich lady in red was on her feet, clearly having made a go at scoring more than one bachelor.

Georgie saw it, too. "One for her son and one for herself? It looks like it's time for you to do a little shopping."

"Four thousand dollars." Kat hadn't stood. Simply and quietly, raising her hand toward the emcee, she'd stated her bid. The only people that heard were her friends, the emcee…and Michael.

The emcee's voice rose with genuine excitement. "The bid is *four* thousand dollars. Yes, you heard me correctly," she added when people started looking at one another in surprise. "Are there any other bids? Fifty-five hundred, anyone? Four thousand dollars is now the bid." She pointed to the lady in red. "Five thousand two hundred? Five thousand?"

The older lady shook her head and took her seat.

The host held her gavel aloft, glancing hopefully around the room. "Four thousand dollars," she stated slowly, pronouncing each syllable with perfect diction, waiting for one last late bid. "Going once…twice…*sold*, to the stunning brunette at table one."

Michael's stare was black ice as he turned his broad shoulders to face Kat directly. Three feet above her on the runway, he seemed a menacing tiger ready to pounce, the twitch in his jaw more prominent than ever.

The emcee leaned down toward Kat, trying to speak above the roar of the many sudden conversations in the room. Kat stood and matched her posture to Michael's, belligerent, her chin jutting slightly and her satiny, thick brown hair swinging just off her shoulders. She looked directly into Michael's cold brown eyes before turning to smile at the host.

"What is your name, please?" the emcee asked.

Katherine approached and spoke her full name into the woman's ear, and she had to hand it to the woman, she was smooth; Carol's only show of surprise was a slightly raised eyebrow. When Ms. Young turned back to the audience, the crowd quieted to hear the name of the person who had paid four thousand dollars for this bachelor.

"The winning bid for Michael Blake goes to…Katherine Blake. The former *Mrs.* Michael Blake."

# # #

Katherine was back in the bathroom. She had negotiated the conclusion of the auction with a reasonable amount of elegant charm, or so her friends suggested, but now reality arrived with a great wave of nausea. Doubling over, Kat clutched at the pain in her stomach. What she was about to do made her physically ill.

Tara pounded on the door of the stall. "Get out here, Kat. Now! You're going to miss the finale, and you still have to pay the committee."

Kat heard Georgi muttering something about her being a chickenshit, so she called from behind the stall door, "I heard that."

"Well, you are," her friend threw back. "Every time you step out of your comfort zone for more than fifty seconds you end up in the bathroom. And this was all your idea. You gotta toughen up or Imodium will be your constant diet for the next week. You're acting as if you're still in love with Michael, not like you had a plan and you're following through."

Kat stepped from her temporary sanctuary and faced her friends. She looked quickly to her left and right to make sure no one else was in the room then turned back to defend herself. "I am not in love with Michael, how many times do I have to tell you that?"

"Until one of us believes it," Tara said. "What exactly are you going to tell him?"

"That I want him to complete the renovations on our house. I can't sell it the way it is, and he knows that. It would cost me a fortune to have someone of his talent come in and finish. Michael shouldn't be surprised, because I tried to get it done before the divorce. He refused. He kept telling me his heart just wasn't in it." She still sounded bitter, even to her own ears.

"Gonna keep him workin' both day and night, huh?" Georgi giggled. "Didn't the emcee tell you not to do that? Remember Carol Young told you to bring him back well-rested."

Kat couldn't even smile. She moved closer to the mirrors, the harsh light turning her skin to a sea-foam green. This was by far the most deceitful thing she had ever done, and guilt was gnawing a hole in her gut.

"I look like a ghost," she said shakily, *and feel like a villainess.* Suddenly the knot in her stomach felt twice as large, and her skin grew paler. "Do either of you have some blush?"

Georgi flipped a lock of strawberry-blond hair from her shoulder and began digging in her handbag. After setting a package of wipes on the counter, a Matchbox car, two pink baby bows and a binky with red and white polka dots, she finally produced a small compact and handed it over.

Kat reached for the case and felt something rubbery on the bottom. She quickly turned it over, afraid of what she might find. "Your blush has a gummy bear stuck to it," she told Georgi as she pulled free a small red glob.

"It's okay, you can eat it. I've got a whole bag full. The kids won't miss one."

Tara and Katherine shared a look, and this time Kat did relax enough to smile. Georgi could almost always lighten the mood, even when she didn't realize she was doing it. She was such a loyal friend, a wonderful wife and the best mom Kat had known since her own mother. A warm surge of love swept over her, and she gave Georgi a tender hug as she handed back the compact.

"Georgi, please tell me this will all be all right. You know how much I want to have a child." It was Georgi and Tara's turn to exchange a glance, but Katherine was quick to reassure them. "Don't worry, you two, I promise I won't fall apart. I've made my decision, and I'm not about to back out now. I realize that my strategy is unorthodox to say the least, and I must admit I'm uncomfortable with how I'm about to carry it out, but all mothers sacrifice for their children. Like you said out there, Georgi, this is my first sacrifice."

Georgi shrugged and began throwing her assortment of mommy survival things back into her oversized shoulder bag. "I can't even comprehend *trying* to get pregnant," she muttered. "Jim and I had one in the crib and one in the oven before we had time to breathe. I honestly don't even remember having sex between the two. Maybe just sleeping in the same bed can get you pregnant, at least after the first kid."

Kat knew in her heart and had for a long, long time that she was meant to have a baby. More importantly still, she'd known that the father should be Michael. She wished now that she had gotten pregnant earlier in their marriage, because then this would all be over. But life had a way of happening on its own terms and in its own time, and now, no matter what had become of their relationship, she was going to create a precious life with the help of her unknowing and unwilling ex-husband.

Chapter Two

Michael had stayed in the dressing room as long as he thought possible without letting on to the other bachelors just how disturbed he was about the scene his ex-wife had created, but now he had her backed up against the wall in the cloakroom. While his physical posture made him feel somewhat better, dominant and overpowering, his emotions proved he wasn't even remotely in control of this situation.

Kat faced him, her hazel eyes locked with his. God, he'd almost forgotten how startlingly beautiful she was, with that smooth complexion and dark hair. She was wearing it longer now; it hung thick and shiny to the tops of her shoulders. Even as angry as he was, Kat's beauty seemed to melt one tiny layer of ice from around his heart.

"What in the hell are you up to?" he hissed.

"Let's discuss it at my house," she replied.

It was this calmness that had infuriated him before the divorce. When she'd quit fighting, quit trying to make it work and simply resigned herself—that made him crazy. "Damn it, talk to me, Katherine. Are you just out getting your kicks with the girls, or are you really out to ruin me?"

"*Ruin* you?" She laughed. "Ruin what, your reputation as the most eligible bachelor on the mountain?"

Michael had an impulse to slap one perfect cheek, but he would never do that. Never had. Instead, he grabbed her elbow and propelled her to the lobby and through the glass doors. His truck was already parked at the curb, and a valet opened the passenger door.

"Get in," he commanded his ex-wife.

"I drove my car," Kat told him, slipping a gloved hand into her coat pocket and producing a parking voucher.

"Get in," he told her again through clenched teeth. "We'll pick your car up tomorrow."

"But—"

He unceremoniously hoisted her with a hand on her butt into the tall vehicle, slammed the door on her protest and walked around to his side of the four-wheel drive Ford. Without another word he slid behind the wheel and was immediately assaulted by the smell of her perfume and clean hair. Damn her, the least she could have done was change shampoos after all this time. This was one of the few moments in his life that he wished he'd taken up smoking.

As he wove through the nearly deserted hilly streets of the old mining town of Park City, he rolled down his window an inch to rid himself of the memories Kat's scent brought back. The frigid night air seeped into his brain, helping him to think more clearly. Katherine stayed silent on the other side of the truck, and he wanted it to stay that way, at least until he could get his anger in check. The two had started their married life on this mountain and he had honestly imagined them living here for the rest of their lives. Together.

He was tired. The holidays seemed so harsh and cruel these days, and he was relieved they were over. Eagle's Nest had been swamped with hundreds of demanding guests. Rooms had somehow been double-booked, and they'd had to find housing elsewhere for irate visitors. They'd had a ski lift break down on Christmas Eve, and to top it all off, it hadn't snowed for ten days and the slopes were getting rough and icy. Every night during the holidays Michael had plodded back to his condo in the corner of the resort, exhausted and depressed. He hadn't even bothered putting up a Christmas tree— hadn't had one, in fact, since Kat put one up two years ago all by herself. He still remembered that night. He had gotten home late, bone-tired, as he had been every day while trying to get the resort up and running. He hadn't even noticed the tree until after he'd finished whining about his work. Now, thinking of that night, he could still see the look of defeat on Kat's face. It wasn't long after Christmas that she'd asked him to leave.

After the last hellish week, the last thing he'd wanted to do was spend New Year's Day with a bunch of women at some damned bachelor auction, but he had committed to Make-A-Wish in a weak moment and never went back on his word. He had been dreading this upcoming week, spending time with some woman he didn't know. He'd hoped he would at least be auctioned to someone who liked to ski, or maybe to some lady who would need him to shovel her walks and do little jobs around her house, the kind of little old lady that fell asleep at eight o'clock at night. Of all the women he had imagined going home with, this one had never entered his mind.

From the corner of his eye, he glanced at Kat's profile in the headlights of a passing car. He couldn't believe how natural it still felt having her sit next to him…but comfortable or not, he wasn't going home with her. He didn't give a tinker's damn if the foundation made him pay back the money she'd spent. He was not going to step one foot in his former home, that charming gingerbread-trimmed house on the hill.

"Okay, Kat, out with it. What's the deal?"

"Homer's been ill for some time now," she stated.

Michael's heart turned over and made a low thump in his chest. Katherine's grandfather was the only grandparent either of them had ever known. Michael missed Homer and his crazy antics almost as much as he had Kat.

"God, Kat, is he going to be all right?"

"He's over the worst of it. He had pneumonia, but at his age I just can't let him stay alone in that old shack of his. Not in the winter. He should be in the retirement community."

"Homer loves that place," Michael said. "And after we fixed it up, it isn't such a shack anymore."

Kat's voice hardened to brick. "Trust you to just brush it off. I should have known better than to think you'd be concerned."

He felt his stomach twist. "That's a shitty accusation. You know how much I care for that old coot. Just because you lose someone doesn't mean you quit loving him. You make me sound like a cold-hearted bastard."

There was a pause before Katherine's deep sigh filled the cab of the truck. "I don't really think that, Michael. I just think…your priorities have changed."

"More than you'll ever know," he muttered.

"Anyway, back to my reason. I need some carpentry work done."

Michael snorted. "You mean you need me for some manual labor? I'm flattered, Kat. But I'm really not that kind of guy." He recognized the old flirtatious tone in Kat's voice.

Kat rolled her eyes and laughed. Now *there* was a sound he hadn't heard in a very long time. His gut tightened further. He figured it was a double knot.

"Oh, brother. You are a piece of work. I'm sorry to shatter your illusions, Valentino, but I'm afraid you're slightly behind the curve. I do need your body, and for a purely physical reason, but it's not what you're suggesting. I want you for hard, sweaty, manual labor."

He nodded his head, knowing he was stepping into muddy water here. What was wrong with him? Why did he want to pick at a scab that had once wounded him so deeply? "That's what I meant too." He gave her a knowing look.

"Michael, listen to me. Read my lips. I don't want you for sex."

"'Sex.' When did you start using that cold term? You used to say that 'sex' was something you did with a stranger—no commitment. 'Making love' was a totally different experience altogether."

"Michael, please." She sounded tired, as if she couldn't keep up a pretense. Or was he reading something into this that wasn't there? Hell, it didn't matter, he supposed. He wasn't falling for this woman ever again, or any of her tricks.

She continued. "Just listen for a minute without trying to be cute or clever."

At that moment, Michael didn't feel cute or clever; concerned and certainly confused, but that about summed it up. "Okay, fine. What kind of manual labor?"

"Homer keeps dropping in to visit. He stays for days at a time, and as you well know I have no room for him to sleep. I need you to finish the two bedrooms in the attic, the ones we didn't get finished before you left."

Michael despised the way she always talked as if he had just walked out one day never to return. "You keep forgetting that I was asked to leave. That was your decision, remember?"

"I don't want to bring up that old argument. Not right now. Can we please just stick to the subject?"

Michael snorted again. Katherine never wanted to bring up an old argument—at least not one that she might have been wrong about, and this was definitely one of those. He pulled up in front of her house and shut off the lights but left the truck's engine running. The house was ablaze with colored Christmas lights. He'd loved Christmas with Kat. They'd made so many dreams together. Dreams that were all dead.

"Okay, back to this scheme of yours," he said, trying to sound like a professional businessman. He hoped his murderous stare straight ahead would let Kat know that he was not going into that house, at least not tonight. "Most of the materials are already in the attic, so why didn't you just hire someone from town? It would have been cheaper than four grand. What's the deal, why me?"

"First of all, it would not be cheaper than four grand and you know it. Secondly, you did a beautiful job with the restoration on the rest of the house, and I want the attic to look the same. Thirdly, you're used to Homer and he's comfortable around you. I really don't want anyone else in, spreading rumors about him all over town."

"So your grandpa is up to his old tricks, is he? He must be feeling quite a bit better," Michael said with a laugh. He felt the knot in his belly loosen somewhat. "That old guy tickles the hell out of me. How old is he now?"

"Eighty-three, with the appetites of a twenty-year old."

"Is he still hitching rides to Salt Lake?"

"I'm afraid so. He hardly ever drives the car you bought him. But his hitchhiking isn't quite as dangerous as it used to be. He's made friends with the UPS driver, and every time the driver delivers a package to my shop Grandpa talks him into taking him to the city, even though it's against company policy. Homer says he likes to ride in a truck with no door; it makes his adrenaline flow."

Michael chuckled again. He still loved hearing Homer stories. "How's his love life these days?" *I'll bet better than mine.*

Katherine sighed. "That's part of the problem. His lady friends won't go with him to his place. They say it's too far from town, so he's always bringing different women back to my place. He's got a new signal. If he comes in with a woman and his baseball hat is on backward, I'm supposed to get lost for an hour or so."

Michael's belly laugh filled the confines of the truck.

"Now do you see why I need you so desperately?"

Michael shook his head. "I can see why Homer needs his own room, but I still don't see how that involves me."

"I've told you all the reasons, Michael. Why won't you believe me?"

"Because I *know* you." He knew this woman better than anyone he'd ever met in this life. She'd only surprised him once, and that was with the divorce papers.

"I've told you everything, Michael."

She sounded as tired as he felt, but: "Bullshit."

Katherine pulled her collar up around her neck. The white fur against her dark hair was breathtaking, so Michael turned his glance away from her.

"Look," she said, a new energy in her voice. "I don't care if you believe me or not. You agreed to be in the auction and work for the highest bidder."

"Yeah, well, I didn't agree to be a slave to my ex-wife for a week."

"The rules didn't say a damn thing about who could buy your services." Michael thought he heard amusement in her voice. Was she enjoying this? She continued, and her tone was even more mocking. "I'll bet you're just crushed that you aren't with Heather right now, aren't you?"

Michael was taken aback. "Who the hell is Heather?"

"You know, the blonde with the big...bangs that bid on you."

"Is that her name? *Heather.*" He tried to make the word sound dreamy. "Poor kid, she seemed like a nice girl. Too bad somebody with a lot more money and an ulterior motive had to show her up."

"You poor baby," Kat said, touching a gloved hand to his cheek. "Just think. You could be in hooter heaven right now."

"Oh, well." He sighed. "There's always next week."

Kat slugged him in the arm then looked him square in the eye. Her sweet tone was laced with a touch of malice. "You can do anything your little heart desires after this week. But for the next seven days, darlin', you're all mine. You wouldn't want to disappoint the Make-A-Wish Foundation or make the scene there would be if I asked for my money back, would you? I can't imagine that'd be good for business."

He raked a hand through his hair. God, he hated this. He was so tired; he just wanted eight hours in bed. His own bed. He'd been doing so much better the past few months, and now this. *Her.* A light dusting of snow covered the windshield.

"I'm not coming in, Kat. I'll sleep at my place and be back early in the morning."

"No. You'll stay here."

"Damn it, Kat. I don't even have any clothes!"

"There are still some of your work clothes in the attic. We'll ride to Eagle's Nest tomorrow and pick up your tools."

"Good hell, you're treating me like a kid," he growled.

"I paid damn good money for you. If you'll recall, you were the one who taught me that. If you pay top dollar, you should expect and receive the very best for your money."

"It's two o'clock in the morning. We're not going to get one thing done tonight. Why can't I sleep at the condo and be here bright and early?"

"Because you'll ditch me. You'll go home and start to think about it, and then you won't come back. I was married to you for eight years, Michael. I did learn a thing or two along the way."

He felt his hackles rise. "'Ditch' is a strong word, Katherine. I never intentionally left you alone. I—"

"Don't worry about all that," she told him lightly, interrupting. "I'm cool about the whole thing. You have your perceptions and I have mine. Believe it or not, I'm really not in this to dredge up old angers. I just need some more space in the house for Homer, and I thought it would be fun to have you help me finish the remodeling."

Fun? She'd thought it would be fun? She was out of her mind!

She sounded sincere and congenial, though. In the dim light of the dashboard he could only make out shadows, but he could hear the smile in her voice. She sounded almost as sweet as when they'd first met. So, why didn't he trust her? Why didn't he believe that she'd forgiven and forgotten? She hadn't given him a reason, and yet he was convinced there was something she wasn't telling him.

Michael sighed and looked at the house again. He let the colors of the Christmas lights blur and become one solid glow. He wondered who had hung them this year, and a jealous twinge made his jaw ache. He recalled the winter evenings that their warmth had welcomed him home, but now those colored lights were an unwelcome reminder of those long, cozy nights when they first moved to Park City. They'd snuggled together in front of the fire and planned the house and their future, believing that they were the happiest couple in the world. When had it all fallen apart? And how?

Katherine's weary voice broke the silence. "Come on, Michael, let's go in. I'm tired."

Michael seriously considered pushing her out of his truck and speeding away. But if he left now, it would look to Kat as if he were afraid of something. He wasn't. Not anymore. He simply did not want to get back into a situation that would cause him discomfort. Talk about a rock and a hard place.

He opened his door then suddenly shut it again. "If I stay, I get the bed."

"You always got the bed in every fight we ever had. It's my house now; you will sleep on the couch."

He opened his door again and stepped out. The night air was cold. He hadn't won five arguments with this woman in eight years. It was nice to know some things never change.

"No," he said, slamming the door behind him. He rounded the truck, jerked her door open and continued his argument. "Do you remember what I always told you about that? I'm never angry enough to sleep on the sofa, and tonight's no different."

Katherine didn't reply. She hurried up the icy sidewalk ahead of him and turned her key in the lock. She was wearing silly high heels, but Michael resisted the old habit of holding on to her to steady her steps. He wasn't through with his tirade yet.

"If you don't want to sleep in the bed with me, fine. Don't. But I'll be damned if I'm going to be miserable all night and work for you all day tomorrow. This is your crazy scheme, Katherine, so you choose. Is it my bed or yours?"

Kat's exasperated glare was the only response he needed. They went in the house but stood in the entryway, staring each other down, chins almost touching.

Finally she turned away, removing her coat and hanging it in the coat closet. Then she kicked off her shoes just as she always had done and walked into the kitchen. Over her shoulder she asked, "Can I get you a drink or some hot cocoa?"

"No." Michael knew his voice sounded harsh in response to her polite offer, but he didn't care. "I'm going to bed." He walked toward the one and only completed bedroom in the house.

"Are you serious?" Kat asked with surprise, sticking her head out from around the corner of the kitchen. "You really do plan on sleeping in my bed?"

"You better believe it."

"Give me a few minutes to get changed first," she said, rushing past him.

She left him standing in the middle of the living room, so he looked around, wondering if anything had changed in the time he'd been gone. If the exterior of the house looked Victorian, all signs of that tradition were left at the front door. He felt the familiar but pleasurable shock of color as he stood in Kat's eclectic world. If the home's workmanship was all his, the decorating was all Kat's.

He set a match to a previously built fire and sat down in a wingback chair next to the hearth. As he did, a memory returned of coming home from work the day Kat had painted two of the walls a deep, rich red. He'd been raised in a house of beige and brown, and he'd thought she was kidding when she told him of her plan. Within a week the mismatched furniture from their previous apartment had been replaced with elegant furnishings in black and white stripes with bright yellow accents. It was outrageous, absurd...but it worked. That was Kat.

Michael rose abruptly. He felt like a cornered cougar as he waited. He hoped to get at least a *few* good hours of sleep before tomorrow. Actually, he hoped he could get to sleep at all. What was taking her so long? He could hear her rummaging in the bathroom that was attached to the master bedroom. His impatience grew.

"Would you hurry up!" he yelled.

"Just a minute," she called in reply.

What was she up to? He wondered again.

Kat entered the living room brushing her thick, silky hair. She knew damn well what *that* did to him.

"Where did you find that shirt?" he asked suspiciously.

She was wearing a man's red and black flannel shirt that hung to the middle of her thighs. She had worn that shirt and nothing else a dozen times during their marriage. He'd loved her in it and she knew it. Michael wanted to kill her. Was she intentionally messing with his head?

Kat looked innocently down at the shirt and began brushing her hair again. "You must have left it when you moved out."

"You know damn well I didn't leave it intentionally. It was your favorite shirt, and I'll bet you hid it so I couldn't find it."

She shrugged. "So what? I bought it for you, I can take it back if I want. What difference does it make now, anyway?"

"None. It makes no difference at all." He walked away from her and into the bedroom.

If he thought nostalgia had moved him in the living room, it threatened to consume him in the bedroom. Everything was just the same. It was as if he'd gone to work that morning and was coming home to sleep that night. Visibly shaken, Michael turned to shut the door and found Katherine standing behind him.

Oh, dear Lord, please make her go away.

His voice came out scratchy. "So, you made your decision. We're going to share the bed just like old times." He prayed that she would recoil at the question, as he didn't think he could do that to himself.

Her gaze slipped past him, and her face suddenly lost all color. With one flying leap, Kat made a swan dive onto the bed, showing a tantalizing flash of lacy black panties. Another smooth move took her to the nightstand where she grabbed something and shoved it inside a pillowcase.

"No," she stated coolly, as if nothing had happened, then began pulling free the comforter and one pillow, which she bundled in her arms. "We're not going to share. I'll take the chaise." Her tone took on a fake Southern drawl. "My mama always taught me to be kind to the hired help."

She left the room carrying her bedding and oozing sexuality, still in his shirt. Michael had feared it earlier, but he was sure of it now: Before the week was over he was going to kill her. He just wished he knew what she was up to.

He stripped off his clothes in a manner of seconds and without thinking crawled in on his former side of the bed. Then he noticed the small gray cover of a thermometer lying on the carpet. He knew instinctively that she had been trying to hide the instrument when she'd made that leap earlier. Could she possibly be sick? Maybe that was why she wanted her grandfather closer to her. Unfortunately,

Michael knew Kat well enough to know that she wouldn't confide in him about her problems at this time in their life.

"Great," he muttered as he crawled under the sheets. "One more thing to worry about."

Chapter Three

Katherine squirmed on the chaise and yanked the comforter up over her shoulder. Apprehension and guilt rolled around in her brain like loose marbles. Maybe she *was* losing her marbles. She'd removed the ovulation kits from the bathroom and hidden them in her underwear drawer, and after a quick scan of the area Kat had felt safe that she'd taken care of any evidence. When she noticed the thermometer lying next to the bed, she almost fainted. She'd have to be much more careful in the future.

She rolled over and tried to find comfort on the small sofa. The fire burned merrily in the hearth beside her as she asked herself again and again the same question that had haunted her for weeks: Could she go through with this plan? It wasn't in her usual nature to be deceitful, but this was different. She had wanted to be a mother her entire life, and her own parents had died before she married. Homer was eighty-three and was the only family member she had left. When Kat had married Michael, their dreams of the future had always included children. Michael had seemed to be as excited about kids as she was. She wondered if he ever thought about all the plans they'd made together and never carried out.

She replayed the evening's events in her head as she lay sleepless in front of the fireplace. Michael was angry, as she'd known he would be. She didn't know what exactly he'd hoped for at the auction, but it wasn't her. The look on his face clearly proved that point. She was honestly surprised at the seething animosity he'd shown—surprised, and slightly flattered that he still felt anything at all for her, even if it was just anger. There was some kind of weird connection still between them, which excited her in a sick sort of way. Didn't they have to be connected if they were going to have a child together? But for the first time she began to wonder if her desire for Michael in her life was actually more than she wanted it to be.

Katherine's stomach tensed as she thought of those dark eyes glaring at her. Those eyes had always revealed so much of what Michael was thinking; he'd had no idea how much they told her about his moods. They were the color of coffee with a teaspoon of cream when he was happy, but tonight they had been just like he drank it: black. He had changed physically too. His dark, barley-colored hair was shorter than she'd ever seen. It made him look sophisticated and polished in a way that threw her nerves off balance.

He'd gained some weight, which didn't make her feel any better. Her ego didn't like the fact that he hadn't wasted away after the divorce. Instead, he looked big, strong and even more foreboding with that etched jaw. His shoulders seemed broader, though his waist still looked as small as it had in college. Without a doubt, Kat knew that Michael didn't want to be here. At all. Realizing that truth made her rethink her plan once more. If he ever found out what she had in mind, he would come unglued.

The big flannel shirt twisted underneath her, and she sat up to straighten it. Her nightwear had provided the effect she wanted: not too much sexuality, but certainly a hint. She smiled in the firelight, remembering that smoldering look in his eyes. That was one emotion she would never forget how to read. Desire. Just the tiniest flicker, but it had been there all the same. He might not want to be here, but Michael had desired her. Was it simply lust, or a small spark from the past? Kat wasn't sure, but it didn't matter. Either would suit her purpose.

His shirt? Kat would never tell the real reasons why she kept it. For one, she couldn't stand thinking of some other woman wearing it. Two, Michael had worn it the last day they lived together as husband and wife. During their argument that fateful night, Michael had taken it off and thrown it in a corner. His smell and the scent of sandalwood still clung to it. She hadn't washed it for weeks but kept it under her pillow during that first long winter alone. Now she wore the shirt because it was warm and comfortable. Nothing more. She was over all the silliness.

With renewed determination, Kat finally fell asleep. She dreamed of cappuccino and her friends. The three of them were laughing at something Georgi was saying about one of her kids. Katherine felt safe and warm, and she snuggled deeper into that comfort and dreamed away until she realized in her groggy state of mind that she was indeed smelling coffee. She hadn't awakened to that wonderful smell for over two years.

Who? she wondered for a moment in her drowsy state, and then… *Michael.*

Her heart lurched forward, as did her body, and she jumped from the couch, waking as she did. Stiffness slowed her down, but she stretched and walked to the kitchen to glance around. Michael wasn't there, but coffee was brewed. An empty mug sat in the sink. She poured herself a cup and sat down at the antique farm table.

A commotion sounded over her head. The attic. Michael wasn't wasting any time. It was obvious he wanted out as soon as possible.

Katherine took a gulp of coffee, burning her tongue. This wasn't going to be as easy as she had hoped. There wasn't *that* much left to do on the two bedrooms upstairs; if he worked fast, he could be done in three or four days. With a deep sigh, Kat resolved that she would work just as hard and hopefully accomplish her goal as well.

She set her mug in the sink next to Michael's and went in search of a hairbrush. As she stroked her hair, she stared at the woman in the mirror. She looked the same in physical terms—ebony hair, straight and thick; hazel eyes, nice figure—yet something had changed so that she hardly recognized herself. Who had she become? She was so desperate to have Michael's child that she had almost lost her identity. Was it truly so important that she needed to lie to him on the off-chance he rejected her request? What had happened to the integrity she always prided herself on?

She stepped back from the mirror, shaking her head. She was making too much of her qualms. She wouldn't back out now; she was too near her objective. She had him here now, so she would go through with it. What he didn't know wouldn't hurt him. He'd made the choice long ago to not be there for their marriage, so he could live with the repercussions of that decision. Somehow that didn't entirely make her feel better as she undid a button on the flannel shirt, slipped on an old pair of Uggs Michael had bought her, and climbed the stairs to the attic.

She entered the first bedroom and stopped dead in her tracks. Her gaze had traveled up the ladder to its third rung, where Michael's bare toes were tightly wrapped around the step. His thick calves were bare as well. A little further up, she recognized an ancient pair of khaki shorts with a torn pocket.

It was obvious that she was going to have to let him go home and get some clothes. He was shirtless, and his broad shoulders and arms had bulked up so much that she doubted the flannel shirt she was wearing would even fit him anymore. He was hammering nails into the casing above the window seat and hadn't noticed her.

"You've been working out, haven't you, Michael?"

He jumped at the sound of her voice, and the ladder swayed slightly. "God, Kat, don't scare me like that. If I kill myself, you'll never get your project finished."

He had no idea just how right he was.

"Sorry," she said, without a hint of sincerity.

"Where's the T-shirt you said was up here?" he asked. "I couldn't find anything but these old shorts, and they're falling apart. I need a shirt, it's colder than a witch's—"

"I'll go turn up the heat and bring back this shirt for you."

"Just take it off and give it to me now," Michael said, looking down at her with an irresistible half grin.

For a split second Kat forgot all their past troubles. She had a vision of them making love on the dusty hardwood floor, and her belly warmed. Shaking her head, though, she regained control. "You'd like that, wouldn't you? Some things never change."

She wanted Michael, yeah, but she also knew how he loved the challenge of the chase. She needed him ripe and ready for the picking, and more than one time. She'd string him along for just a few more hours to get him good and revved up.

"You know what your grandpa says about that. 'If you're too old to look, you're better off dead.'"

Kat wasn't about to get into Homerisms this early in the morning. Her grandfather had a saying or a joke for every subject known to humankind. "Do you want some breakfast? I can make some toast and jam."

"Well, that's better than nothing. And get me some more coffee. I'm not used to such late nights. And a couple of other things," Michael continued, "if you're going to keep me caged up here for a week, you're going to have to buy some real food. I'm not going to live on that birdseed you call food."

"Yes, sir." Kat saluted, standing to attention. Then she eyed him with authority. "Just remember who's in charge this week, Mr. Blake. Me!"

"Don't start with that bullshit or I'll come down there and spank you."

"Only if I ask you to," she purred.

He suddenly looked uncomfortable. "Very cute, smartass," he muttered, hammering in a two-inch nail with two whacks. "Go get dressed. I'll drop you off at your car. Then I've got to go to the resort so that I can get my tools and some decent work clothes while you go get groceries. This afternoon I want to see the football game, so I'm warning you right now, I'm taking some time off."

"Michael," she said softly. "You're doing it again. Watch my lips."

He glanced down at her, and this time his eyes traveled the length of her body, pausing on the shadow of cleavage revealed by her strategically undone buttons. His eyes clouded, and he abruptly raised his gaze to her mouth. "I'm watching," he stated coldly.

"You are not in charge."

Michael just hammered in another nail with a swift stroke.

Kat turned away. As she descended the stairs, she heard him mutter something about flannel shirts and lasagna. *Lasagna?* That one word stopped her dead in her tracks. She hadn't made the dish since Michael left. The word brought a slow throb to the pit of her stomach, and a flood of memories: The night had been cold and snowy, much like today. She had spent all day in the kitchen then lit candles and slipped into Michael's flannel shirt and nothing else. She could still see the raw emotion and desire in his velvety, brown eyes when he'd walked into the house from work. Dinner forgotten for the next hour, but when their other appetites were satisfied, they had shared a huge plate of lasagna in bed.

Kat's hesitation returned as the bittersweet pain the memory caused threatened to consume her. For another moment she stood on the stairs, reliving the power of the love they had once shared. It was obvious Michael was remembering, too. She wondered what the recollection did to him.

Damn it, she couldn't allow herself to think about the past. It would ruin her plans for the future if she let herself get emotionally involved. After everything they'd been through, after the past two years, it just couldn't happen. They both knew it, and that was that. She was simply seeing to her plan to have his child.

She was on the bottom stair when—before she knew it or could stop them—the words flew out of her mouth. Kat yelled up to Michael, "I'll fix lasagna for dinner."

Chapter Four

Michael returned from Eagle's Nest with a tool belt and a duffel bag of work clothes. As he entered Katherine's home, the tangy aroma of tomato sauce and garlic assaulted him. He fought off the memory it brought. Outside, a north wind had turned the temperature to near zero, and in contrast the toasty home air wrapped around him like a handmade quilt. The weather reports were suggesting the biggest blizzard of the season was headed their way.

"Kat," he called, moving to the antique armoire that concealed the television when not in use. He was just in time for the football game. "I'm back." He turned the television on, flipped channels and listened for a second to a pre-game spotlight. When Kat didn't appear, he went in search of her.

"Can I help with anything?" he asked, stepping into the kitchen.

She was standing at the sink taking a pill. She almost choked on it, and hurriedly she slipped the pill bottle into the pocket of her apron. "No thanks," she said, turning to face him. "Everything's fixed and the lasagna is in the oven. We'll eat after the game."

Michael stood staring at her.

"What?" she asked.

"Are you okay?"

"Sure," she said, but sounding not at all sure. "I'm all right. Why do you ask?"

"I just wondered if you might be ill."

"Ill?" Her voice came out in a squeak. "Do I look sick to you?"

Michael stepped a little closer and raised a hand to her cheek. Her flesh felt warm on the back of his hand.

"You do look a little flushed. Are you sure you're not coming down with something?"

She shrugged, clearly uncomfortable. "I'm fine, really. Come on, the game's probably starting. Go take a seat."

When he was installed in the other room, Kat surprised him by bringing out a tray of all of his favorite junk food, chips, dips and plenty of hot salsa.

"What's all this?" he asked.

"It wouldn't be a football game without them, would it? I had fun at the store."

Michael was on the striped couch, and Kat cuddled up in a blanket on the chaise in the other corner of the room. The two of them cheered and yelled for their favorite team, the Broncos. He had always loved watching sports with her. She became outrageously blunt when she got involved in a game. Kat had grown up in a family of men and knew more about most sports than he did. They had once made a habit of watching games together. That had been a long time ago.

He watched Kat jump from her chair when her favorite running back ran eighty-nine yards for a touchdown.

"What a stupid call," she shouted at the television a few minutes later. "That wasn't pass interference. Fifteen yards *now*? From *there*?"

Michael grinned and got to his feet. "Want anything while I'm up?"

"A Diet Coke with ice would be great, thanks."

He left the room whistling softly.

# # #

This feels nice, Kat thought. Very nice. Watching Michael head off to get her drink, she had to remind herself not to get too comfortable. They were not walking back into a life together. That hadn't been part of the plan, because it wasn't something that could conceivably happen. She had to keep her goals realistic.

When the game ended, she went into the kitchen to set the table. Michael leaned casually against a doorframe, watching. He seemed relaxed and content, and perhaps that warm look in his eye meant he was revved up enough for her purposes. Maybe this was the perfect time to give him a hint that she was indeed interested in something more than carpentry work. If they could kindle a healthy sexual relationship for the next week, that would be her best chance of getting pregnant.

She leaned over the table and lit two tall candles, switched off the light and walked over to his chair, pulling it out for him. "Dinner is served," she said.

He walked over to stand beside her, looked down into her eyes with an expression that was both exciting and scary. He wanted to kiss her, was going to kiss her—and for one crazy minute she didn't want him to.

What was she thinking? Of *course* she wanted him to. This was all part of the seduction plot.

Yet, the fear was strong.

If I let him kiss me, I'll lose myself to him again. I can't let that happen. I must be in charge of the situation. I must take control, and then I will feel nothing.

Kat stood on tiptoes and brushed her mouth across his lower lip. She let her eyes flutter shut as she took in the sweetness of his breath, and they stood still for a brief moment. The nearness of him was familiar and yet brand-new.

He kissed her back in a rush of hot red heat, and her knees buckled.

Oh, sweet heaven. I'm not controlling this.

"Smells like I'm just in time for supper!"

The boisterous voice was followed by a slam of the front door. Michael and Kat, dazed by emotion, stood motionless; then suddenly they moved apart as if somebody had just yelled "Fire!"

A man in his mid-eighties burst through the kitchen door with the speed and energy of a much younger person. The white hair sticking out from under a baseball cap and the slight slump to his shoulders were the only hints that gave away his age. "Well, Holy Toledo, who woulda thought. How ya doin' there, kid?" he asked, extending his hand to Michael.

"Just fine, Homer. And yourself?"

"I'm good, real good. At least, that's what all the ladies tell me," he said with a wink.

Kat disguised her irritation by setting another place for dinner. When she was done, she flipped on the light with a touch of hostility. She loved her grandpa dearly. He was her mentor, but sometimes…

"Let's eat." Looking at Homer, she realized she hadn't even said hello. "Grandpa, where's my hug?"

She embraced him, feeling like a little girl again. Grandpa was Old Spice and comfort, even if he had the worst timing.

They sat down, and Kat dished up large portions of lasagna, stringy with mozzarella cheese. "Grandpa, how did you get up here from Salt Lake this time?" she asked, eyeing Homer suspiciously.

Her grandfather ignored her and turned to Michael. "I hate it when she gives me that evil eye. Her grandma used to do the very same thing. It makes me feel like a ten-year-old that cheats on his arithmetic." He dug excitedly into his square of lasagna before continuing. "I caught a ride with a friend."

"What friend?"

"Ernie."

"Ernie who? I've never heard you talk about an Ernie."

"I don't know his last name. He drives a truck for E.A. Miller."

"When did you meet him?"

Homer took a long time swallowing before answering. "Tonight."

Michael shook his head and grinned.

Kat sighed. "You were hitchhiking again, weren't you?" She didn't wait for his response. "Does the retirement home know you're gone?"

"Probably. It's boring when I'm not there."

"Oh, Grandpa," Kat said, shaking her head. "It scares me to death when you take off like that without letting somebody know."

"It's a retirement home, not a nursing home. I can come and go as I please."

"I know that, but hitchhiking is so dangerous. And when you don't let the home know you're leaving and you don't tell me you're on your way… It could be days before we even knew you were missing!"

"Kat's right, Homer," Michael said, surprising her. "Why don't you get that cataract surgery done so that you can drive again?"

"Because women my age are lookin' rough as a bleached out piece of wood. With cataracts, they still look pretty good!"

Michael laughed aloud, and Kat even found herself amused.

"We don't want you hitchhiking again, Homer. Please," Michael said.

The word *we* didn't pass by Kat. Her heart skipped once like a scratched CD.

Michael continued. "From now on, if you want to come to Kat's, you call me at Eagle's Nest and I'll come get you. If I'm busy, I'll send someone else after you. Okay?"

Homer grimaced. "Why does everyone talk to me like I'm a child? I'm eighty-three years old. I've been around the block once or twice. I'm not senile, and I'm not stupid."

"Then don't do a stupid thing like hitchhiking." Michael held his stare and didn't back down.

"Okay, okay, you win. I'll just ride with people I know. Did you see the game, kid?"

Kat sat back and watched. Homer had been calling Michael *kid* since the first time they met, when he'd practically been a kid, and she knew Michael loved him. Michael's own father had walked out on him and his mother before Michael could even walk. By the time he turned thirteen his mother had died from cancer. Homer had been the only male figure other than teachers and coaches in his entire life.

"Yes, we watched it here."

There was that *we* again. Kat shivered.

"I watched the first half, and Ernie and I listened to the second in his semi. Ernie's a football fan, too. So, you two playin' house again?"

Michael choked on his water.

"Grandpa!" Kat said, also taken aback by the abrupt change in topic, and by his bluntness.

"Well, it looks pretty cozy in here to me. I always knew the angels connected you two in another life somewhere, but sometimes you lose sight of Heaven and you have to stop and look for the stars again. No shame in that."

Kat rose restlessly and began to clear the table. Usually her grandpa's insights were right when it came to her and Michael, and she wondered what exactly he was implying. She stole a glance at Michael and saw he looked as uncomfortable as she felt.

"In the fifty-two years your grandma and I were married, we must have lost sight of Heaven a hundred times or more. She could be a crabby ol' gal. But one of us always gave in, and we'd look to the dark sky and see a dim light and then another and another until the whole black universe was glowing with sparkles. You can't stay mad or hurt with a sky full of diamonds over your head. What's for dessert?"

Her throat full of sentiment, Kat couldn't speak. She opened the fridge door and wished she were tiny enough to crawl inside. How would Homer feel about her plans to get pregnant with Michael's baby and then move away and never tell him? She looked blankly at the shelves, not remembering what she was looking for.

Disappointment. That would be a gross understatement of her grandfather's feelings. And she couldn't keep it from him. Wherever she went, Homer would follow. Kat knew without a doubt that he would love the baby unconditionally, but how would he feel about his granddaughter and her decision to be so unfair?

"Cherry cheesecake," she heard herself say. "Cherry cheesecake is dessert."

She cut the two men each a generous piece but none for herself. She felt nauseated, and she wasn't even pregnant…yet.

Chapter Five

Michael snuggled sleepily against a warm back and pulled the covers up over both of them. His senses were awakening and he could smell…Old Spice. Disgusted, he turned onto his other side and tried to go back to sleep. At least Homer wasn't snoring anymore. All night his breathy wheeze had kept Michael staring at a ceiling he couldn't see in the dark.

He had just dozed off when the snoring began again. The alarm clock read 5:55. Michael blinked his eyes and groaned.

Kat used to play a silly game. If you looked at the clock and the numbers were all the same, like 11:11, you got to make a wish and it supposedly came true.

"I wish to wake up in my own bed and find the last two days were only a nightmare."

Michael rose, went into the bathroom and turned on the shower. He had insisted on the shower when they'd remodeled, although the big bathroom held a purple claw foot tub with brass fixtures. His eyes strayed to that briefly, but he wouldn't allow himself the pleasure of erotic reminiscence. He was tired and too damn mad right now to remember frolics in bubbles.

The hot water eased the knots in his neck and shoulders. At least Kat had given him back the pillows and blankets she'd taken. He wondered if she would have done if her grandfather hadn't been sleeping with him.

Still fuming and wearing only a towel, Michael walked into the living room and began shaking Kat's exposed right shoulder. She lay sound asleep on the chaise.

"Kat, wake up."

She turned away, groaning softly.

"Damn it, Kat, wake up." He turned on the lamp over her head.

"What is your problem?"

"*You're* my problem."

"Take two aspirin and call me in the morning." She rolled onto her stomach and put a pillow over her head.

Michael yanked it off. "Let's get going on this project of yours."

Kat's eyes flew open. She looked surprised, seeing his bare chest and wet hair. For a moment her expression got soft and it appeared she was going to say something, but Michael just waited, glowering. After a moment, Michael got impatient.

"Look, if I can't sleep, you can't sleep. Get up and get dressed. Let's start poundin' nails."

"Pounding nails," she repeated. "What fun."

# # #

Kat took her time in the shower. She thought she'd give Michael a spell to work off his frustration, what with him having a hammer in his hand. Her biggest concern at the moment was her grandfather.

It would have been so easy earlier, what with Michael standing over her in just a towel. If Homer hadn't been in her room, she could have simply led Michael to her bed and had sex with him five or six times. But Homer was here, and she couldn't hurt his feelings by asking him to leave. She didn't even dare offer him a ride back to his retirement home for fear of making him feel unwelcome. But, somehow she had to get rid of him. Tomorrow could be the day she ovulated. Her temperature readings were dropping slightly. She didn't want to miss her chance.

She got out of the shower, dressed in jeans and a sweatshirt, went downstairs and poured two glasses of orange juice. Bearing them, she walked slowly up the stairs to the attic. Michael was puttying nail holes in the trim of the smaller of the two bedrooms.

"Have you got the paint for this room?" he asked over his shoulder.

"I've got the blue, but I'll have to run to the store and buy the white." They had always planned to use this room as the nursery. Kat was determined to complete the room as they had once intended. She'd start a new life with her child here. Maybe she would eventually sell the house, but she couldn't part with it yet. That was asking too much. But she would have to leave before Michael learned what had happened.

"What do you plan on doing in here—or do I dare ask?"

"I'm going to paint the ceiling like a March sky with billowy clouds."

Michael's body stilled, and she could see the tension in his shoulders and back. "Rona told me you've been seeing some guy from Salt Lake. Things must be getting serious if you're finishing the nursery."

His tone was biting, and Kat couldn't help but respond in kind. "I thought Rona was your secretary, not your private detective. Don't get me wrong, Michael, you know I adore Rona and everything she means to you, but she's listening to the wrong people this time."

Michael turned. The muscle in his jaw was ticking again, and he threw down his hammer with a thud. The echo of metal on wood was deafening. Kat held her breath, watching his eyes turn to black chips of coal. She knew the next words out of her mouth would determine whether he walked out or not. At another time and place she might have enjoyed making him jealous, but this was neither. It had been a long time since such games ended happily.

After careful consideration, Kat decided on honesty. At least partial honesty. "No, Michael, I'm not seeing anyone. Rona must have me confused with someone else. And as far as the nursery…" She looked around the room and sighed deeply. "Who knows, maybe someday someone else's baby will wake up every morning to a blue sky."

Michael's eyes were misty like hers, and Kat suddenly realized she wasn't lying at all. Her baby would never sleep in this room, not when it brought such memories for both of them. It was really too bad that Michael wouldn't be the husband she'd always wanted, could only be a father in secrecy and deception.

She had to get out of the room, away from any more questions and Michael's probing, dusky eyes. "I'll go get breakfast. Homer always wakes up starving."

"I don't doubt that," Michael said as she left. "I'll bet he works off three thousand calories sawing logs every night."

Her grandfather was already in the kitchen as Katherine came down the stairs. He greeted her with a cheerful smile.

"I started some bacon."

"Good morning, Grandpa," she said, somewhat subdued.

He walked over and gave her a bear hug. "Like my new hat?" It was a bright red baseball cap that said E. A. MILLER MEAT PACKING. Homer had over a thousand baseball hats, and he cherished every one of them.

"It's a beauty, Gramps. Let me guess," Kat added, smiling for the first time that morning. "Ernie gave it to you."

"Right off his old bald head."

"How did you sleep?"

Homer went back to tending the bacon, making room as she began to prepare eggs. "Slept like the dead. If I could bottle that deep sleep, I'd be a millionaire."

"What's this about no sleep?" Michael asked, coming down the stairs.

Kat shot him a look. "Grandpa was just telling me how well he slept."

Michael got the message and didn't complain, but she could see in his eye that he'd never spend a night in bed with her grandfather again. "Nice hat, Homer. How many do you have in your collection now?"

"Fourteen hundred and nine," Kat's grandfather stated proudly. "A feller can't have too many hats."

"Fourteen hundred and nine?" Michael repeated. "What are you *ever* going to do with that many?"

Homer put the bacon on a paper towel to drain and pulled up a chair, turned it around, straddled it and rested his elbows on the back. "I've got it all planned out," he said, his faded gray eyes twinkling. "I need fifty-one more. I've got to have all of them before my eighty-seventh birthday. Then, on that day I start wearin' a different hat every day. It'll take me four years to wear them all, and on my ninety-first birthday I can die."

"Grandpa, don't talk like that!" Kat scolded.

"Well, good hell, woman, do ya want me to hang around till I'm two hundred? I'd like to see your grandma again before she forgets how handsome I am."

"What happens if you don't die on your ninety-first birthday?" Michael asked.

"Then somebody better damn well buy me a hat!"

Four years from now, Kat thought. Would her little boy or girl be old enough to remember their great-grandpa? She would help the baby remember, with stories and pictures and hats—hundreds and hundreds of hats. A child should know its family.

Oh, God, what was she doing? She was already putting too much hope on this whole damn scheme working. And, what *about* family? Didn't a child have every right in the world to know its father as well?

Kat set plates of bacon and eggs and toast in front of the two men and walked out of the room. Why, she wondered, did she always get these feelings of all-consuming guilt at mealtimes? She wouldn't keep up her strength if this kept happening.

Sitting down on the couch, she stared into the fireplace, thinking. So deep was she in reflection, she didn't notice Homer until he sat down next to her. His arm went around her shoulders and he pulled her close.

Kat rested her head against his chest and gave in to the sheer comfort of having someone care. "Oh, Grandpa," she sighed. "How did you ever survive the loneliness after Grandma died?"

His answer surprised her: "That's what people don't understand, honey. You don't survive. You die right along with them. Then one morning, the one that's left behind is reborn. You learn to walk and talk and laugh all over again. It's a slow process, as slow as when you're a baby. If you try to hurry the procedure, you fall on your face. You've got to start on a tricycle and work your way to a ten-speed."

Kat listened carefully, not saying a thing.

"But, Kat..." Her grandfather hesitated. "Michael didn't die. He's in the kitchen eating his fourth piece of toast right now. God is giving you another chance. Take the ball and head for the end zone."

"You don't understand," she said, pulling away. "He isn't here because he wants to be. I bought him for a week at an auction. Forced him into it. Disgusting, huh?"

"I know all about it," her grandfather said with a smile. "I read the paper, dear. Why do you think I hitched a ride up here?"

"I bought him," she repeated. She didn't like the way that sounded, even to her own ears. "I bought him to...to remodel the house. And when he's finished, I'll never see him again." She was whispering as tears spilled down her cheeks. Why was she crying? It wasn't Michael that was making her cry, though. It was her grandfather's words. She was crying because she wanted a love like her grandpa and grandma had shared. She didn't want to spend the rest of her life alone, with or without a child.

She wanted love.

To be honest, she wanted Michael's love.

Damn it.

Chapter Six

Kat took Homer downtown with her. She'd only gotten some rudimentary shopping done yesterday, and if a blizzard was coming like the weather reports claimed, she needed to pick up a bit more. Just in case. Plus, the grocery store was one of her grandfather's favorite places to pick up women.

"I'll get my own cart and start at the other end of the store if you don't mind," he announced as they arrived.

"Grandpa, we've been through this a dozen times. When you're staying with me, you don't have to buy your own food."

"I know, but...I guess you're old enough to know the real reason." He leaned over and whispered in her ear. "You cramp my style."

"Is that so?" she said. She couldn't hold back a grin.

He nodded his red-capped head. "It's true. I'm afraid the ladies see me with you and think that I'm going after the younger fluff. It discourages them."

Kat shook her head in amazement. "Okay Grandpa, I'll pretend like I don't know you. But meet me at the car in a half hour. I've still got to buy paint and stop at Laurelwood for a minute."

Homer checked his watch and nodded. "One hour."

"One *half* hour," she said.

She passed him in the bread aisle. Homer was asking an older lady with red hair something about seven grains. Two aisles later, he was lecturing a stunning woman with silvery hair on the benefits of Metamucil. Kat doubled back and picked up a few last items.

Her basket full of all Michael's favorite foods, she paid for her purchases. A cold blast of air hit her face as she pushed outside, moving her cart quickly to her car and opening the trunk. It was starting to snow. It seemed a blizzard might indeed hit, and she hoped to get the rest of her errands done beforehand. She got in the car and sat down to wait.

Homer didn't appear. After fifteen minutes, she walked back to the store to search for him. She walked the aisles three times before finally giving up. She was worried sick, yet somewhere in the back of her mind she knew he was all right. He had done this before; she supposed either a redhead or a silver-haired beauty had been talked into driving him home. But just to be sure, she sped back to the house and gave up on the rest of her errands.

When she stepped in the front door, Michael was the only one there to greet her.

"Hi, where are the groceries?"

"They're still in the car. Have you heard from Homer?"

"Yeah, he just left."

She fought back annoyance. "Left for where, with who?"

"Somebody named Celeste. A silver-haired lady. He said she was an old friend he ran into at the supermarket." Michael looked at Kat and then it dawned on him. "Oh. He didn't know her before today."

"Right."

Michael shook his head. "I need a page out of that man's book. He's fast, he's smooth."

Kat rolled her eyes, pleased at least that her grandpa was okay. And she'd wanted him out of the house, so maybe this was a blessing in disguise. "When did he say he'd be back?"

"He said they were going to dinner and then dancing down in Salt Lake. He told me to tell you that he'd see you in a couple of days and that—let me think how he worded this—'your goal posts are in sight.' Do you know what he's talking about?"

Take the ball and head for the end zone, honey.

Maybe she had been wrong after all. Maybe her grandfather had perfect timing.

Chapter Seven

Before nightfall it was snowing in earnest. The wind howled like something out of a horror movie, but inside Kat's home it was warm and cozy. The fire hissed and crackled in the marble hearth. She had prepared a favorite recipe of her grandmother's, homemade chicken soup, to be served with whole wheat rolls.

She was feeling very domestic, actually. That was a change. Maybe it had been her thoughts of motherhood, or maybe it was the simple fact that there was someone to cook for again. Or maybe it was the storm: Blustery, cold nights always made her crave hot soup, toasty fires, soft downy fabrics and—

"We're in for it," Michael called as he opened the back door, a load of firewood cradled in his arms. His head and eyebrows were covered in a white layer of fluffy snow. "It must be zero or colder out there, and the wind is blowing at about forty knots."

He shook the snow from his hair and stomped the slush from his boots onto the rag rug. "It smells delicious in here. Do I have time to call the resort before dinner? I need to have the guys take a few precautions. If the wind is this strong here, it could be roaring at a hundred miles an hour on top of the mountain."

"Make your call. We can eat anytime," Kat assured him.

She watched Michael shed his winter gear and hang it on the brass hooks in the back corner of the kitchen. He exuded a potent energy. He'd always loved changes in weather; the more drastic the better. He came alive with the drama.

As Kat studied her ex-husband, his enthusiasm seemed to transfer to her. The more she thought, the more excited she became.

She turned to the sink and looked out at the swirling and dancing snow. The blizzard was an answer to her prayers.

"Keep it up, Mother Nature. For all I care, you can snow for a week."

They were halfway through dinner when the lights flickered, dimmed, momentarily surged back to life, and then went out entirely. The ensuing silence was as dark as the room.

Michael and Kat sat only inches apart. She'd heard his quick intake of breath at the exact same time she'd felt her own chest expand. It wasn't that a power outage was shocking; the power went out several times a winter in Park City. It was more the surprise—and the memories of other times when the same thing had happened. Times with Michael. Nights they had lit candles all over the house and crawled into the purple tub together.

There came a noise from outside, and they jumped at the same time, accidentally bumping heads. The thud echoed through the quiet.

"Ouch!" Kat exclaimed.

"I've always said you were hard-headed," Michael muttered in the blackness. She was sure his head was ringing too.

"I'll get a flashlight," Kat said. She couldn't see anything. As she took a step, her foot hit something and she was thrown off-balance. Giving a little squeal she fell with an ungraceful thud into Michael's lap. In order to support the unexpected weight, his arms surged immediately around her waist.

She relished the blackness at that moment. Thank goodness Michael couldn't see the color rising in her cheeks.

"Just dropping by?" he asked.

"I'm sorry," Kat told him.

"I'm not."

Flustered, she wasn't sure how to respond. She tried to stand, pressing her hands to his shoulders. "I don't know why I'm so clumsy."

He held her fast. "What's the hurry?" His voice was scratchy.

Kat turned instinctively toward him, her breast pressed firmly against his chest. Michael responded. He buried one hand in the thick hair at the nape of her neck and gently pushed her head down to his. The storm was really making everything easy.

Their lips brushed each other. It was a simple contact; expecting nothing and everything. Then Michael added pressure and heat, moving his mouth over hers, lip scraping her teeth, and Kat felt desire for him rise from her toes, through her thighs, and come to rest in the very center of her. She squirmed on his lap and felt him harden beneath her.

She began to kiss him back, and her passion only grew. Wave after wave of ecstasy surged through her. In her muddled state, Kat wondered who had invented kissing, and she wanted to place a call through the ages and thank desperately whomever it was. She marveled at the electricity that rushed through her at Michael's touch. Why did no other man make her feel this passionate? Thoughts of the few clumsy kisses she'd endured since the divorce made her want to laugh and cry at the same time.

It finally ended. Michael released his hold and untangled his fingers from her hair. Kat made to rise, and this time she encountered no resistance. She was full of sadness, and neither of them spoke. Katherine's heart pounded against her chest, and a wave of terror filled her. She wondered if Michael felt the same. If he was as frightened as she by their intensity, she knew why he had ended the kiss. She had to regain control. This was everything she didn't want. She wanted a child not complications.

Kat made her way to the kitchen counter and reached for the drawer that held the flashlight. She took two breaths. In no time at all, tiny flutters of candlelight dotted the room.

"Finish your soup," she commanded Michael softly, trying to cover her vulnerability. "I'll light some candles in the living room."

A phone began to ring as she returned to the kitchen.

"That always startles me when the power's out," she told Michael, picking up her cell. "Hello?"

"How's my little darlin' tonight?"

It was Homer's sunny voice. "I'm fine, Grandpa. How are you?"

"Peachier than a peach. Are you all tucked in up there? Kevin says it's going to be the biggest storm of the year."

Homer was on a first-name basis with all the television news people in Salt Lake, although he'd never met one of them. Kevin was the weatherman on Homer's favorite station.

"We're tucked in," she assured him. "In fact, we were just having a bowl of Grandma's chicken noodle soup."

"Are you sure that's safe to eat, honey?" Homer asked. "She must have made it a hell of a long time ago. She's been dead fourteen years."

Kat laughed. "Where are you, anyway? I'd like to throttle you for skipping out on me at the store."

"So, is the Kid still there?"

"Yes, Grandpa." Kat twisted the cord with her fingers. She looked over at Michael, leaning lazily in his chair. The candlelight made his eyes sparkle. "Now answer my question. Where are you?"

"Celeste invited me to her senior-citizen Zumba class."

She didn't think that's where he was. Not now. "I thought you were going dancing and to dinner."

"That's what she told me, but dinner was some lettuce and junk in a flat piece of bread with a pocket in it, and dancing was jumping around at a health club with a bunch of saggy—"

"Grandpa!"

"Well, hell! Every one of those ol' gals was wearing a jogging suit. Nobody wore that tight, shiny stuff, and not one of them looked even a little like Jane Fonda."

"I thought Celeste was beautiful, Homer. Is she nice?"

"Oh yeah, but I'm taking it upon myself to teach her about the finer things in life—like a juicy steak and slow dancing."

"I'm sure you can do it. Now, for the third time, where are you?"

"At the Kennel."

She breathed a sigh of relief, as that was what he called the retirement home. He'd be safe for the storm. "And where is Celeste?"

"She went to her apartment in Sandy. It's her night to host Bunco."

"In this storm?" Kat asked. "Well, you please stay put until the weather passes. Do you promise?"

"Must be a bad connection. Guess I'd better hang up now."

"Homer T. Reynolds." Kat used her firmest voice. "Don't leave the home again until it quits snowing. I'm serious about this. I've got enough on my mind without worrying about your safety right now. Go find your friend Bill and have a hot game of chess."

"Don't ever put the words 'hot' and 'Bill' in the same sentence again. And Bill's so damn slow at chess he has to wake me up every time it's my turn."

"Then get some of the girls to play bridge, watch a movie, or go to bed, but don't leave there. Please," she added.

"Don't want me up there ruining the mood, huh?"

She breathed a sigh of relief. "Exactly." He'd swallow that much more easily than her being worried about his safety.

"Why didn't you just say that? Haven't I always told you the truth is easier to take?"

"That's not always right, Grandpa."

"Now, don't argue with me, young lady. I've been walkin' the trail for fifty-five years longer than you. And, this applies to you and the Kid, too. You keep something from him, and you're liable to end up changing your own flat tires for the rest of your sorry life. Remember."

Kat suddenly felt Michael's eyes upon her. Her lip trembled and she turned away, whispering to Homer, hoping Michael wouldn't hear. "I can change my own flat tire, Grandpa."

"Yeah, but it ain't no fun."

That was her grandfather's last word on the subject. As she set down her phone, Kat's cell phone beeped and signaled a text. She knew it wasn't her grandfather, because he didn't know how to text. The message was from Georgi.

R U BUSY??? HOPE SO! LOL.

#

After they learned via a transistor radio that the power could possibly be out for several hours, Michael called Eagle's Nest and was reassured by Rona that everything was running as smoothly as possible. His secretary was a godsend.

"Chef Louie has even risen to the occasion and prepared a feast of cold cuts. Actually, most of the guests are enchanted by the whole eighteenth-century atmosphere. We're just fine. How are *you?* All cozy and warm, Michael?"

There was no mistaking the quiet hint of suggestion in the woman's voice, and he wondered how much she'd guessed. Michael's thoughts raced back to the kiss. The power of it flooded his system again.

"Surviving." He tried to sound nonchalant.

Kat was clearing the table. From the way she clattered the bowls in the sink, she must have put two and two together and guessed the question he'd been asked. His answer had ticked her off and he knew it. Maybe *surviving* had been an inappropriate choice. Michael wished he could snatch it back.

"Well, Kat's ready to do the dishes, guess I'd better help." The comment didn't help. Kat shot him another dark look.

"Okay," Rona conceded. "But, Michael, remember tomorrow. You need to be here no later than nine. They'll be here at ten."

"Nine, right. I'll see you then."

"Nine when?" Kat asked in a clipped tone as Michael hung up. She was ready for a fight and he could tell.

"Nine tomorrow. I'm sorry, Kat, but I've got some VIPs coming in and I've got to be at Eagle's Nest. I figured that whoever bought me would be accommodating if…" He trailed off, realizing how the situation mirrored their past problems, him always putting work first. If she'd only understood what he was trying to accomplish, they would never have broken down so badly.

"Great," she retorted. "I can be accommodating. Who are these very important people?"

He felt his hackles rise. "Calm down, Kat. Jealousy doesn't become you."

"Your arrogance isn't attractive either, Michael. The only thing I'm jealous of is your time. I want my house finished."

"Are you sure that's all?" he snapped. "For some reason I still don't believe you."

"It really doesn't concern me what you believe. You are supposed to help me for a week. Your *very important people* will just have to get along without you." Her bitterness was palpable.

"Look," Michael said, raking a hand through his hair. "I made it clear to the committee before I joined the auction that I had this event, and because it also involves the Make-A-Wish Foundation they were fine with it. It's not my fault that they forgot to tell you. Regardless, I have to be there."

Kat was silent. The pain in her face made Michael ache, and he shook his head and gave a sigh. He supposed he would try to ease the situation.

"Let's drop it for a while. We aren't getting anywhere arguing like this. I'll do up these dishes so we can relax."

"Forget the dishes," she said. "I'll do them tomorrow." Her tone was still very cool.

Michael sighed again and pushed the light on his wristwatch. Only seven-fifteen, too early for bed. It wouldn't have been too early for bed at another time in their lives together, but this was not that time. Even if he *were* willing to take the risk of suggesting what his body desired—which he wasn't—Kat wouldn't likely consider it. Not now. Not after that reminder of the past.

Restless, he wandered into the living room, picked up a candle, and scanned the bookshelves for something to read. "Kat, do you know whatever happened to that spy novel I was reading the day you kicked me out? I've always wondered how it ended."

Kat stomped into the room, pushed past him, grabbed a book from the shelf and threw it at him. "Kicked you out?" she said, glaring. "You're really chalking up the points tonight, and you have a very convenient memory. I simply told you that things weren't working as they were, and that if we couldn't work them out it would be better if you left. You literally jumped at the chance."

"I think you're the one with the convenient memory, Kat. If I had left by my own choice, why did I feel like someone ripped my guts out?"

As soon as Michael made his admission, he wished he hadn't. Kat looked up sharply, an expression of surprise crossing her features. Her face softened a little then clouded once more.

"If I kicked you out, why did I feel utterly destroyed?"

Was that possible? Michael wondered why neither had ever spoken about their feelings before now. Had they really both been too hard-headed to tell the other what they were thinking? Was this his fault?

"How the hell was I supposed to know what you were thinking?" he asked.

"At the time you didn't give a damn," Kat shot back. "Not about what I was thinking or feeling."

They stood head to head, hearts pounding. Not touching, not moving, barely breathing.

Michael felt hot wax from the candle he held drop down onto his thumb and blister his flesh. He ignored it.

God, he'd never thought to hear Kat admit they might have made a mistake. If they could only erase the last two years. But it had taken him a long time to get over his addiction to Katherine Blake, and that kiss earlier had been like taking a first drink after two years of sobriety. She'd been the hardest habit he'd ever had to break. Why had he taken that drink? He wasn't sure he could survive the anguish of losing her again. He stood apart from her, saying nothing.

But, it was too late. He wanted her so badly—wanted to hold her forever, to show her in a thousand different ways that he was sorry and could make it all better. She filled his body and soul with sheer uncontrollable passion. He took a step toward her.

Kat took a step backward. "I'm going to take a bath before the hot water's gone," she told him quietly, so quietly that he had to strain to hear. Then she turned and walked away.

Once more scalding wax fell to Michael's fingers. He welcomed the pain. He picked up the spy novel and tried to find his place. It was impossible to concentrate.

The bedroom door shut softly behind Kat. Left alone in the room, Michael set the candle down, put a couple of logs on the fire and picked up the book again. Someone had turned down the corner of a page, and he found that it was the last page he had read. He wondered, curiously, if Kat had possibly hoped that he might return some day to finish it.

"It doesn't really matter. It's too late, anyway," he heard Kat say in his mind. He supposed that was true.

Michael listened to the bathwater running and tried to concentrate once more on the book. He heard Kat's deliberate movements and he knew she was undressing. He read the same sentence three times. As the first splashes of water sounded and then a deep sigh, his imagination went wild. Slamming the book shut, Michael strode to the bathroom and flung open the door.

"Abe Lincoln might have done it, but I can't!" he huffed.

"Done what?" Kat asked, pulling a few fluffy bubbles up to her chest.

Michael was awestruck at the sight of her, candles shining all around, hair pulled high on her head, water and suds lapping at her breasts.

Eventually he found his voice. "Read by candlelight."

Kat smiled. It was a slow smile, seductive. Michael had seen it before, knew just what it meant. But he couldn't believe he was seeing it now, not after what had happened outside. He felt like he was being bounced back and forth like a ping-pong ball.

"I know what you mean," she murmured. "Candlelight should be used for *other* things." Her palms swayed gracefully in the water, like the branches of a willow. Michael swallowed hard. It seemed like she was inviting him to join her.

"Did you use all of the hot water, or did you save some for me?"

She looked like a little girl who had just taken the last cookie from the jar but didn't feel a bit bad about it. Brushing a lock of hair from her forehead with the back of her hand, she removed all doubt about her invitation. "If you want a hot bath, you'd better get in now."

Crazy or not, he couldn't resist. He wasn't going to wait for her to change her mind, either. At this moment he didn't give a damn about the consequences. He'd worry about those later.

What was wrong with a little fling, anyway? Hell, she was his ex-wife. He'd only had sex once since their divorce, and that had been a total disaster. He had subconsciously compared the poor woman to Kat all night, and the tryst had ended very badly. Kat owed him one, damn it, and now was time to collect.

Within seconds Michael had removed his clothing and was standing next to the tub. After all this time he should have been embarrassed at his nakedness, but he wasn't. Kat didn't seem disturbed, either.

"This is your last chance, Katherine. If I get in this tub, there's no telling what might happen. Are you willing to take the risk?"

A smile lifting one corner of her mouth, she whispered her response. "I am if you are."

# # #

Kat prayed Michael couldn't hear her knees banging together. The water was hot, but she shivered with nervousness. What had she done?

She pulled her legs up to her chest and wrapped her arms around them, and Michael stepped in beside her. He was calf-deep in the water, and the nearness of his bare physique sent excitement through her. She'd had no idea he would crash in here like he had, but she supposed that meant her plan was fated to succeed. Just before her bath Kat had used the ovulation kit, and she believed the timing was perfect. She wanted to believe the universe was conspiring for her.

Michael slid down into the steamy suds. "It's hot," he said, catching his breath.

Kat wondered if sperm could be killed by water that was too hot. "Let's add some cold," she suggested.

Michael grimaced, trying to maneuver his legs alongside Kat's. "Since the tap is buried in my back, I don't think that's such a good idea."

His toes brushed her hips. They were facing each other now, seesaw-style. Kat tried to look calm, but it was tough when she knew that within a few short minutes they would be on their way to making a baby.

Michael seemed relaxed. She supposed this was commonplace to him, bathing with women—likely snow bunnies such as that bimbo Heather from the auction. Wasn't that what he was doing up there in Eagle's Nest? She couldn't imagine him not taking advantage of his success and reputation, a success she had watched him build while she waited at home for him. She was about to be just another in his long line of his conquests, regardless of the fact that she'd been dumped after eight years of marriage. Her blood boiled, but her smile remained plastered to her face. She would have the last laugh. This was all about her plan.

She silently spoke to her preconceived baby. *This one's for you.*

Her arms slipped off her legs. Steeling her nerves, she slid forward until she was boldly sitting on Michael's lap, her legs wrapped around his back. At the feel, all anger drained away. God, she loved the textures of him: smooth and rough, soft and hard. She ran her tongue up and down the curve of his jaw, his two-day scruff like an erotic sandpaper.

Michael shivered. He cupped her breast and rubbed the tip with his thumb, and when Kat arched forward he bent down and slipped the nipple into his mouth. His desire was blatantly apparent now, and Kat reveled in it. She cradled Michael's head in her arms while he ravished her breasts and wondered, startled, when the seducer had become the seduced. She took the opportunity to regain control and begin explorations of her own.

"Oh, Kat," Michael whispered. "This feels so damn good, to be in your arms again. I've missed you."

Molten sensations dragged her in and out of coherent thought. His lips came up to her neck and found the certain spot that only he knew about. Shutting her eyes, she breathed deeply of the scent of him, that heady aroma of sandalwood and soap she'd missed since he left. How good things had once been, how beautiful, how perfect. She could feel he was ready to give her everything she wanted. She was drowning in pleasure and happiness.

Lazily she opened her eyes. Candle flames dotted the room, some short, some long. The muted light and silence apart from the lapping water wrapped them in a dreamlike state. Kat could see the back of Michael in the vanity mirror, and her own dark head behind his. She felt his hands on her hips, moving her, repositioning her—

Suddenly, Kat's languid eyes flew open and her body stiffened in terror. On the counter, just below the mirror, was the ovulation kit!

She tried to relax so that Michael wouldn't know something was wrong. How could she remove the kit before he saw it? He was muttering something between kisses about finding a more comfortable place. That gave her an idea.

"Yes, yes," she agreed breathlessly. "Take me to bed."

They stood, never parting their lips, tongues or hands. It would have been wonderful, but she absolutely had to get him out of this room.

Michael stepped out and down from the high tub then lifted Kat by the waist. Setting her beside him, he drew her back into his embrace. They stood for a moment longer, groping each other like teenage virgins.

Kat was scooped into his arms then, and like Rhett carrying Scarlett, Michael crossed the room. They were almost home free when he stopped dead in his tracks. Katherine looked up to his face and followed his eyes to the vanity. Her heart stopped. Completely. Michael was stone still, and his expression unreadable.

"Look at us, Kat," he said very slowly. "Turn and look in the mirror. We look so damn good together. I want you to remember this moment for the rest of your life." Then he swept her into the next room and laid her on the bed.

She needed a jump-start on her heart. He hadn't seen the kit. *Thank you, God.* It was the universe conspiring. She'd just have to excuse herself as soon as they were through and get rid of the evidence.

Both of them were still damp. Michael pulled a sheet over their bodies and began his seduction in earnest. When it came right down to it, Kat couldn't believe how smoothly this was going. How perfectly. Her previous tension eased, and she began to rediscover her earlier pleasure.

Michael explored every inch of her with his mouth and fingers, and in turn she returned the favor. It wasn't long before she was back on the brink of ecstasy.

"Michael," she moaned, clutching at his head. "Please, don't torment me any longer. Come to me, now. Please." She could barely think.

Michael lifted himself along her body. She opened herself to him, barely able to make out his features in the dim light, but his need for her was apparent. She knew his release would be as powerful as her own.

Taking him in her hand, she guided him toward fulfillment. But just when they should have connected in the strongest physical way, Michael pulled back. He spoke for the first time in several minutes, and his words were choked with passion.

"I'll be right back, babe. Don't move."

Babe. He'd used to call her that. She doubted he'd even realized the endearment slipped out; but before Kat could think about the implications, Michael was gone and in the bathroom with the door shut!

What in the hell was he doing? Had he seen the kit when they were in the bathroom earlier? Had he taken her to the edge of delirium only to drop her cold for revenge? And if he hadn't seen the kit before, would he notice it now?

She heard drawers opening and closing. God, what was he looking for, more evidence of her deception? Kat thought of running from the room—the *house*—to avoid his wrath, but it was her house and she had nowhere else to go. Especially not in a blizzard. She could still hear the wind howling outside. It gave voice to her fears.

With great apprehension, Kat waited for the door to open. When it did, she was amazed at the expression on Michael's face. His eyes were still filled with desire, and he was carrying a string of tiny foil packets.

"I found some!" he said triumphantly. "I thought I'd left some in one of those drawers." Three seconds later he was in bed and wearing a condom.

Good God, Kat thought. Where was a pin when you needed one?

How could there still be condoms lying around after all this time? She wanted to scream her frustration. At the same time, she wanted to laugh at the absurdity of the whole damn mess.

Michael took her gently in his arms once more, and she melted under his careful touch. Tomorrow she would throw every damn condom away. Right now she would enjoy Michael. It would not be a hardship.

His expert fingers and tongue brought her back to life almost instantly. All concerns were forgotten as visions of Michael and only Michael swirled in her head and her heart. Her body cried with joy at his attention. She wanted him, baby or no baby. And she had him. Fully. Deeply. Completely.

They were each experts on the other's body, and they hadn't forgotten how to pleasure each other; those lessons were burned with fire into Kat's brain. The pair reached their zenith simultaneously, and it was a joyous consummation. She could remember none better.

She lay next to him in a drowsy sleep, marveling at the tranquility he evoked in her, at the fulfillment he was able to bring her in bed. Michael had been the first man she had ever loved; he was the best man she had ever known. If only their life together had worked out, Kat would have been totally content. But their problems were still present, she reminded herself. Even tonight they had argued about events at his resort, and she knew that in the morning she would again lose the battle. He would go to the mountain and place his needs before hers.

Yet, right now, he was here and sleeping in her arms. That was a beautiful thing.

She tapped him gently on the shoulder, and Michael seemed to be thinking the same thing. He turned to her and they began the captivating process of rediscovering each other's bodies.

They made love three more times. Each time Michael used protection, and Katherine remained silent. There was always tomorrow. She was convinced there would be a tomorrow, and she'd throw away any remaining Trojans in the morning. They'd used up the ones he'd retrieved.

She fell asleep with images of a blond-haired, twinkling-eyed baby in her head. Michael was holding the child in his lap.

Chapter Eight

Kat woke early the next morning, slipped into Michael's flannel shirt then threw the ovulation kit and a few final condoms in the garbage. From the looks of her charts and temperature readings, tonight and tomorrow were the best hope for pregnancy this month, though she knew there was still chance of error.

Sometime during the previous night the electricity had been restored, and it seemed the blizzard had been less devastating than predicted. The roads were fine. Kat decided to drop the issue about Michael leaving for the day, pinning her hopes instead on that evening. She felt sure he would return to make love to her again, and she'd just have to trust her instincts. They had stepped into a new realm last night, but the progress might vanish with one mistaken word. She'd be damned if it would all fall apart because of past disappointments.

Georgi texted. It was short and sweet:

HOW WAS YOUR NIGHT? I HEARD THE POWER WAS OUT UP THERE FOR HOURS. NICE GOING. DO U HAVE A SPECIAL DEAL WITH MOTHER NATURE?

"I wish," Kat said aloud as she padded into the kitchen and made Michael a huge breakfast. Pancakes, sausage, eggs, coffee. He was always ravenous after a night of intense lovemaking.

She put two forks on the tray and entered the bedroom. Setting the food on the nightstand, Kat gently woke Michael with a kiss on his bare shoulder. He turned slowly and opened one sleepy brown eye and then the other. Reaching out, he wrapped his arms tightly around her, buried his face in her hair.

"Good morning, vixen." He released her, stretched like a great lion and then groaned, craning his neck. "I'm crippled. What did you do to me last night?"

"Only what you said you needed, Michael, that's all." Kat snuggled deeper into his warmth. "Are you getting too old for a night like that?"

"Did I act old?" he asked.

"Not in the least. I have a feeling you're going to be like Homer, still going strong at ninety."

"Do you think Homer and Celeste—?"

Kat cut him off. "I don't like to think about it."

"Well, I do," Michael said, leaning up on his elbow. "Every man wants to think that he can perform until his dying day. And your grandfather has lots of women flocking around him.

You know they're not sticking around for his jokes."

Kat shook her head, not willing to consider that. "I'm afraid Grandpa is just trying to feed a need my grandma left when she died. It really has nothing to do with sex. They loved each other so much, I don't think he's ever gotten over her—not enough to give his heart to someone else. His flirting worries me sometimes, because I know he'll never be able to commit to anyone again."

"Do you think commitment is required for sex?" Michael asked. "And why should he commit? He's eighty-three. He can just play around for the rest of his life."

"Is that a reasonable solution?"

"Not for me, but I'm not eighty-three."

"I believe that almost everyone wants true, unconditional love, no matter how old they are. They deserve it, even. I want him to have that magic once more in his life, Michael." Kat was suddenly desperate to change the subject. "Now, sit up. I brought us breakfast in bed."

"Smells delicious. I'm famished."

Kat smiled. "I knew you would be."

"Where's yours?"

"You're sharing."

"My shirt, my breakfast…," he grumbled good-naturedly.

"You got it."

"Kat?" he began, and she heard the hesitation in his voice. "I really don't have a choice about today. I've *got* to be at the resort. I hope the crew has had time to groom the trails after the blizzard last night. For that matter, I hope I can get to the mountain."

"You'll be able to," she replied. "I checked the news. And it's okay. I should go over to the shop for a while to make sure everything's okay."

Was that disappointment in his eyes? Had he expected an argument?

"Do you have to go today?" he said after a moment. "I was hoping that you could come with me."

A bite of pancake lodged in her throat. "You want me to go with you to meet your VIPs?"

"Yeah," he said, revealing that boyish grin she adored. "They'll love you."

Suddenly suspicious she asked, "Just who are these people, anyway?"

"It's a surprise. Please come, Kat. It'll be fun, I promise. Wear your ski gear, we'll be outside all day."

She had to admit, if only to herself, that the prospect of spending a day with Michael outside in the fresh snow held great appeal. "Okay," she conceded. "But you owe me one."

"Works for me," he declared. Then, giving a devilish grin, he tucked into breakfast. They both ate in companionable silence.

When they were done, he kissed the tip of her nose. "Thanks for breakfast. It was great. And because it was so good, dinner tonight is on me. I'm going to grab a quick shower. We need to be out of here by eight-thirty. Can you be ready?"

Kat looked at the clock on the wall. "Sure, if you won't hog the bathroom."

He grinned again. "That shower was made for two, remember? I'll get the water going."

Kat picked up the tray and took it back to the kitchen. She was putting the dishes in the dishwasher when she heard the front door open.

"Katherine!"

Homer? Thankful for the modesty of Michael's shirt, she pushed her head out into the living room. There stood her grandfather with the attractive, silver-haired lady he had met in the grocery store. Kat couldn't help but remember Michael's previous comments. Had these two spent the night together? Why had they come up here so early in the morning?

"There you are! Honey, I'd like you to meet my new friend, Celeste."

"How do you do, Celeste?" Kat came out and shook the woman's hand then quickly dropped her arm back to her side and pulled down the short shirt. "You two drove up the mountain this morning? I didn't think the pass would be open yet. Parley's is such a dangerous canyon to drive through, even without a blizzard. I hear a report of an accident almost daily."

"Michael invited us to go with you today," Homer said. "So we got up at the butt-crack of dawn."

Kat fought back surprise. How long ago had Michael invited them? How long had he been planning whatever was going to happen today, and were these the VIPs he'd mentioned? Just what exactly was her ex-husband up to? "Make yourself at home please, Celeste. Homer can get you some coffee while I get dressed."

Worried that Michael hadn't heard the door and would come traipsing out in a towel, or less, she headed toward the back of the house.

"Where's the Kid?" Homer called.

Pretending not to hear, Kat shot to the bedroom and shut the door behind her.

"Michael," she whispered, opening the shower door. He was washing his hair and hadn't heard. When he rinsed the shampoo out of his eyes and saw her standing there, he jumped and yelled, "Good hell, don't do that!"

"Shh! Homer and his lady friend are in the other room."

"Now?" Michael asked, incredulous. He shut off the shower and stepped out, dripping wet. "You've got to be kidding."

"I wish I were."

"Well, I invited him to help us today, but I assumed he'd meet us at the resort. Maybe he got lucky last night too. Like I was saying."

Kat grabbed the damp towel he was wrapping around his waist and flicked him on the butt. Then she handed it back. "Get dressed and go entertain while I get showered."

He left the bathroom. As he did, Kat found herself realizing how easy it would be to slip back into the routine of being a couple. These past couple days had been nice, and the sex had been incredible. How was she going to feel when the week was over? She showered and dressed then went to join her guests.

Michael stood next to the hearth, and Celeste and Homer were sitting next to each other on the couch. Homer had his arm around Celeste's shoulders. The lady was truly beautiful. Regal, slender, and tall, she had thick silvery hair cut in a modern, blunt style. Kat guessed her to be in her late sixties. It was obvious that she had taken great care of herself over the years.

"I'm so glad Grandpa brought you to meet us." She'd said *us* before she could catch herself. There was that couple thing again. "Where are you from?"

"I have a home in Salt Lake and a condo up here." Her voice was rich and warm, and Kat liked her immediately. "I apologize for barging in on you so early. We could have met you on the mountain, but your grandfather insisted on stopping for a minute before we went to pick up our ski clothes."

Kat slid a sideways glance at her grandpa. She knew why he had stopped by so early, and she wondered if Celeste was beginning to get the picture. He was a curious old coot, and he wanted to see exactly how things were progressing.

Her grandfather affirmed her supposition by saying, "I needed to talk to the Kid about some passes, anyway."

"Passes?" Michael asked, not missing the innuendo. Homer had never been subtle. "Oh, you mean ski passes."

"I won't need one, Homer," Celeste said. "I already have a season pass at Eagle's Nest."

"That's why you looked so familiar," said Michael. "I've seen you at the resort."

"I've been skiing since I was five years old, and if I had my way I'd ski every day until I die."

Kat was startled. "Are you ill?"

"No," Celeste said, laughing, "but when you get my age, you want to live life to its fullest."

"You aren't old," Michael replied, obviously taken with the woman.

"I'm seventy-four, dear. That's not exactly in my prime."

Michael and Kat exchanged glances. Clearly neither of them would have ever pegged her as that old.

"Well," Michael said, "Kat and I have to be up to the resort by nine. If you'll follow us to the office, I'll fill you in on the details of

82

the day. We can swing by anywhere you want if you have to pick up ski clothes."

"That would be perfect. Thank you," Celeste said.

"See?" Homer spoke up, giving his lady friend's hand a little squeeze. "I told you Michael was a good kid, and by the way, this'll save me a truckload of money. One month's social security check couldn't cover a day's skiing at Eagle's Nest."

Michael rose from his chair, smiling wryly. "Who said anything about getting you in free, Homer?"

"Come on, kid, be a sport. This could be the last enjoyable activity of my measly life."

"I doubt that, old man." Michael laughed. "I doubt that very much."

"You two, don't worry about us," Celeste said. "Go finish getting ready. Homer and I can entertain ourselves."

"You bet we can," Homer said mischievously, turning his baseball hat around backward on his head.

Kat and Michael went to retrieve the things they needed for the day. As Kat slipped back into the kitchen, she heard Homer ask Celeste, "Honey, do you know the difference between sex and a ham sandwich?"

The woman paused. "No."

"Boy, would I like to take *you* to lunch."

# # #

Kat and Michael drove the last few miles to Eagle's Nest in companionable silence.

The storm was ended. Pure snow hung from branches everywhere, bending them toward the ground with heavy burdens. Everywhere lay deep, fluffy, glittering snow, untouched. The world looked clean again, as if God had freshly painted it in vibrant colors of white and rich pine green, the sky a brilliant turquoise blue.

The narrow winding road led them out of the valley, higher and higher up the mountain until they crested the peak of Eagle's Nest. The resort had been a vision of Michael's since he and Kat hiked to the summit years earlier. That first day, they had spent hours at the high elevation scheming and planning, and Michael had never let the dream die. He had spent his entire life, so far, learning every detail of running a ski resort from the ground up. He'd searched the world for investors that believed in him and his project, and finally he'd won the capital he needed to make his dream a reality. Kat felt a swell of pride. It had been their dream together, and even if the resort had been an instigator of their demise, she still believed in the project.

As the lodge came into sight, she was sure Michael experienced the same pride. Eagle's Nest, named for the enormous bald eagle habitat in the area, sprawled over a thousand acres; the main log structure sat alone on five in the middle. It consisted of a lobby, four gift shops, three restaurants, a convenience store, two ski-wear stores, a complete gym with adjoining indoor and outdoor pools and hot tubs, and fifty hotel rooms. Antique reproductions dotted the structure's wide halls and vestibules. Huge rock fireplaces welcomed skiers into warmth like the hug of an old friend. The building's foyers were immense, and their heavy pine timbers gave the place a grand feeling.

After two unprecedented years of success, Eagle's Nest was the ideal location to escape the pressures of life. It held all the luxuries without much hype. The ski trails were remarkably well suited for every type of skier, from novice slopes to downhill courses that challenged the best of the best. Condominiums snuggled up next to the lobby. Other businesses had leased land and built an elegant little city behind. Art galleries, furriers, ski shops and eating establishments all gleaned revenue from the success of the resort. Movie stars and tycoons now owned private estates along the road to

Eagle's Nest. Many of them loved the Park City area so much that they had opted to raise their families here and commute to the metropolis cities.

As they turned the last corner on the road to the top, Kat remembered vividly back to the time when nothing was here but trees and sky and earth. It was sad, in a way, losing that pristine space, but she also knew that Michael had brought this place to the people so that they too could feel the soul of the mountain. It was a beautiful dream.

"There's the bus now," Michael said as they parked. He walked around and opened Kat's door to let her out. "We shouldn't have stopped with Celeste and Homer to get their stuff. I should have gotten here sooner. Rona will be having a fit."

Kat stepped from the vehicle and turned toward the bus he pointed out. After the storm of the night before, the weather had completely changed. The day was dazzling bright, sunlight glistening off the snowy slopes covered in their fresh coat of virgin snow. She hated the thought of spending such a beautiful day with VIPs, surely a bunch of spoiled socialites, but Michael had wanted her here so she'd make the sacrifice.

Fascinated surprise overtook her as the bus door opened. A mechanical platform emerged, lowering a little girl with a wheelchair to the snow-packed ground. Michael rushed quickly to her aid, but she expertly rolled from the platform and moved to one side.

"Good morning!" Michael said, giving the child a tender smile that brought a lump to Kat's throat. "I'm Michael. We're so happy that you could come to Eagle's Nest to play with us."

The sound of the platform making its slow descent once again kept Kat from hearing the girl's response. This time, a boy of about fifteen disembarked. The process happened over and over again, until at last ten kids and their chaperones were lined up in the cold winter sun.

Rona, Michael's longtime friend and the main administrative assistant of Eagle's Nest emerged from the entrance. The middle-aged woman was dressed in florescent green skiwear and said to Michael with a scolding undertone, "There you are. I thought I was going to have to deal with this myself. Jason called in sick, and the Picabo Lift is down this morning so I had to send Tom and Phil up there to fix it."

"I brought Kat to help," Michael replied, smiling. "I knew the kids would love her."

Rona gave Kat a glance that gleamed with mischievous delight.

"Okay, everybody, listen up." Michael turned to his guests, and his voice held intense excitement. Kat knew the kids absorbed that exhilaration, but she had no idea how he planned to help these handicapped children have a delightful day in the snow. All but two of them were in wheelchairs, and those two wore heavy braces and crutches. Not one of them was wearing more than a light jacket, jeans, and tennis shoes. She wondered how their parents could send them up here without proper winter attire.

"The first thing planned for today is to serve you a hot breakfast. We've got a nice room all set up for you with plenty of pancakes and Captain Crunch," Michael called out. The kids cheered. "Then we'll get you each dressed in some warm clothes and take you back outside for a day in the sun. Does that sound okay?"

The children nodded and all began talking at once. Michael responded to those he could, then chose one boy in a chair and led the charge up the ramps to the lobby. The others followed.

Kat turned a questioning glance to Rona. "Where are these kids from?" she asked.

"Today is from Mesa, Arizona. This is the twentieth group Michael's arranged through the Make-A-Wish-Foundation. That's why he consented to do that stupid bachelor auction, actually. He invites a group a month from all over the country. He pays for everyone's flight, bus transportation and hotel in Salt Lake, all to have them here for a day of fun. When the snow's crummy or it's a bad day for outdoor activities he finds alternate things for them to do. The kids absolutely love him."

Kat let Rona's words wash over her again as she headed up the ramp and into the resort. *"The kids absolutely love him."*

As they headed toward a private dining area in back, Kat saw Homer and Celeste appear. She'd almost forgotten about them. Homer stood silently with his hands in his pockets watching the kids heading toward their breakfast. He was wearing a brand-new purple ball cap that read EAGLE'S NEST in embroidered silver writing.

"Looks like you've got a rewarding day ahead of you," he said, uncommonly hushed.

Kat nodded. Then she had a moment of inspiration, remembering what Rona had said outside. "Grandpa, I hate to ask you to give up your day of skiing, but I was wondering if you and Celeste would help us out with the children. Michael has a lift down this morning and that's left him a little short on assistants. Would you mind helping out?"

Homer's weathered features softened, and he suddenly looked ten years younger. "Sure, we'd be glad to help if you need us. Won't we, Celeste? Michael said he had a project up here."

Celeste nodded. "We'd love to help."

They walked into a dining room full of children's bubbling laughter. Kat thought there wasn't a sound in the world quite so enchanting and uplifting. When Michael saw them, he moved over to the trio and unexpectedly put his arm around Kat and gave her a quick hug.

"Aren't they great?"

His eyes were a sumptuous brown with gold flecks this morning, and she had never wanted to be a part of his life more. She was again choked with emotion and simply nodded her head.

"Homer, Celeste," Michael acknowledged. "Would you like to join us for breakfast? We have plenty. Let's eat!"

He took Kat's hand and led her to a table at the front of the room. The simple contact sent her senses spinning. He pulled out her chair for her and then sat down beside her. Leaning close, he whispered intimately in her ear.

"Thank you for coming, Kat. It means a lot to me."

She didn't respond. Her heart was full of new respect for Michael, and that scared her even more than the passion they had.

A waiter put a hot plate with an omelet, hash browns and toast in front of her.

"Michael," Kat said in a low voice. "We've already eaten breakfast, remember?"

"How could I forget?" he asked with a private smile. "Eat a little," he suggested, picking up his fork. "You'll need the energy later on."

Kat didn't know if he was referring to helping the children or for later on that night.

"Homer," Michael said as Kat's grandfather sat down. "Nice hat."

"Yep. Saw it in one of your gift shops and just had to have it. You've got 'em priced a little high, though. 'Course, everything is priced high up here. A fella would have to sell his virtue to stay here for a week."

"Don't let Homer give you a hard time, Michael," Celeste chimed in. "He didn't pay for that hat. He told the clerk that he was your grandfather and to put it on your tab. He also told her that he personally looked over every application before you hired someone, and that he remembered recommending her for the position."

Michael shook his head and bit into some toast. "Doesn't surprise me at all."

They quickly finished their meal and led their guests to the rental area where Michael arranged for several employees to help dress the children in skiwear. Kat was amazed at how organized and orderly things progressed. Each child had his or her name on a stack of clothes already selected in their size. There was someone available to help each dress, and they were all ready to go outside in a matter of minutes. The group looked bright and beautiful in the brilliant colors.

It wasn't long before everyone had been loaded onto a huge horse-drawn sleigh. The cheeks and noses of the children turned to frosty pinks, and their grins were evidence enough of their enjoyment. The Clydesdales wore sleigh bells around their girths, and the combination of the clomp of their heavy hooves and the tinkling of bells rang through the crystal-clear morning. Homer took out an ancient harmonica he'd had since childhood and began to play. The kids were spellbound.

Michael sat next to a boy with popping brown eyes.

"These horses are cool. Are they yours, Michael?"

"Yes, they are," Michael replied. "The one on the left is Tom, and the one on the right is Jerry."

"Just like the old cartoon, huh?"

"Yes. What's your name?"

"Jesse R. Staples."

"Pleased to meet you, Jesse R. Staples," Michael said, shaking the boy's hand. "How old are you?"

"I'm eleven years old and proud of it." He jutted his chin out, and the smile he offered was similarly defiant. "My dad taught me to say my age with pride because the doctors said I'd never live to the age of five. I've already doubled the odds."

Kat saw Michael's eyes cloud briefly before he replied. "That's wonderful, Jesse. With your attitude I'll bet you buck a lot of odds. Just what is your disease?"

"I have spina bifida. I didn't talk until I was three, and then my mom says since that day I haven't shut up. And I couldn't walk until I was six, but that's okay, 'cause the doctors told me I'd never do that either. I still use crutches most of the time, but when somebody walks with me I can just hold on to them."

"You are a remarkable young man, Mr. Staples," Michael pronounced. "What are you going to be when you grow up?"

"I've thought about being a disc jockey, but I'm really getting into the whole computer thing now so I'm thinking about doing something with them."

"I think you'd be wonderful at anything you decide to do. Tell you what. Why don't you keep in touch the next few years, and I'll see what I can do to help you get into a good university."

Jesse's eyes got bigger. "Wow, that'd be awesome. I just had a feeling this was going to be my lucky day."

Michael and Kat looked at each other over his head. Gazes meeting, they smiled. Kat couldn't help but think that Jesse wasn't the only one having a lucky day.

The sleigh wove through fifty-foot pines and then out to an open meadow. Jesse seemed anxious for more.

"Can these horses go any faster?" he asked, a gleam in his eye. "I feel the need for speed."

Michael laughed. "Let 'em loose, Jeff," he told the driver.

The sleigh gave a slight lurch, and they were off rushing through the meadow like a hawk in pursuit of its dinner. The children all squealed with delight then moaned when the driver slowed the pace back to a trot. Michael was quick to reassure them.

"Don't worry, kids, we'll be doing plenty of fun things today. Next up is a ride on the ski lift."

"A ski lift ride?" Jesse asked. "That's all? I've wanted to ski my whole life."

Kat saw sorrow in Michael's eyes, but as quickly as it came it was gone again, replaced with a quiet determination. "Well, Mr. Jesse R. Staples, I guess this is your lucky day."

# # #

Jesse R. Staples sat snugly on the ski lift, one hand holding Kat's, the other gripping Michael's. Shiny new skis dangled from his feet. Michael had assigned every child helpers according to his or her needs. He and Kat would take care of Jesse for the rest of the day.

"Wow, this is high up here, but not as high as the airplane. Yesterday was my first ride ever in a plane."

"Did you enjoy that?" Kat asked.

"It made my belly feel weird for a minute, but I loved it."

Michael felt Jesse's hand begin to shake, and the boy asked, "What happens when we get to the top?"

"Try to relax your body, and Kat and I will lift you off. If you let us help you, it should be easy."

The closer they got to the top of the ridge, the more anxious Jesse became. Michael turned his head toward Kat and searched her dark eyes, silently asking if she thought they could pull this off. He'd been determined to see this through, but he also saw that they were taking a risk. Still, it was worth it to see the boy happy.

Kat put her arm around Jesse's shoulders and gave him a reassuring hug. "Don't worry about a thing, honey. Michael is the best ski instructor in Utah, and we'd never let anything happen to you."

Michael felt his confidence returning with Kat's praise. The boy relaxed a little, and when they reached the top their exit was remarkably smooth.

Michael chose the safest route possible with the least amount of traffic. They started down the mountain with Kat and Michael on each side of Jesse, holding him tightly. Jesse didn't have the strength or flexibility to ski on his own, but he had a raw determination that warmed Michael from the inside out. Skiing three abreast, the trio made their way to the bottom of the hill. Jesse didn't speak unless one of them asked him a question, and then he simply said, "I'm okay."

They were almost to the base of the run when a rude skier cut them off with a spray of powder. Jesse's body jerked to one side to avoid getting a face full of snow, and the sudden movement sent all three of them tumbling.

Michael reached Jesse first, his lungs bursting in his chest with worry and from the exertion of kicking off his skis and running over. Kat was right behind, panting just as hard. Jesse was lying flat on his back in two feet of downy powder, staring up at the sky.

"Jesse," Michael gasped. "Jesse?"

The boy blinked once and said, "That was awesome! I can't wait to tell the other kids I skied and *crashed!*"

Michael sat down with a thump, relief making him weak.

Kat started to giggle. She fell to her knees beside them, and soon all three were laughing and replaying the whole ordeal.

"Are you all right, Jesse?" Michael asked.

"I'm great. Didn't hurt at all. This snow is like falling into a bunch of feathers."

They helped him upright, brushed each other off, put on their skis and finished the course.

Jesse begged to go again. This time he loosened up and really enjoyed himself, and then they went a third time. By the end of that, he was visibly exhausted. It was a long course, top to bottom.

"One more time?" he asked hopefully.

"Sorry, bud," Michael said, tousling his hair. "You've worn me right out, and we've got to get back to the others. They're probably ready for lunch. Aren't you hungry?"

Jesse nodded. "I'm so hungry I could eat a horse."

They returned to the lodge, where they found the rest of the group already having lunch. The trio joined the others, devouring fries, thick hamburgers, and thicker milkshakes. The others there were happily discussing their snowmobile rides, but Jesse soon became the star attraction as he told the fascinated crowd of his adventures on the slopes.

Michael was always amazed at the genuine affection he found the children had for each other. There was no animosity among them, and these kids were genuinely thrilled that Jesse had gotten a chance to ski.

He felt Kat take his hand, and she applied a little pressure. "This is a wonderful thing you're doing, Michael Blake. I'm proud to know you."

He glanced over at her and looked deep into her eyes. Those eyes had melted his heart over ten years ago, and now he felt it happening again.

"It's the most rewarding thing I've ever been a part of," he confessed. He suddenly wanted to ask Kat how she felt about their relationship after these past few days together, but this wasn't the right time or place. How long, in the back of his mind, had he been hoping for a chance of reconciliation?

"Grandpa Homer," a little blonde girl with a tiny deformed body and beautiful blue eyes called out. "Play us another song?"

Sometime during the morning Homer had become Grandpa to these kids. Michael considered asking the man to be Grandpa to *all* the groups that came to play at Eagle's Nest from now on.

Homer pulled the old harmonica from his pocket once again and danced and swirled with shuffling elderly feet to the rousing tune of

"Five Foot Two." The performance brought the house down, although Michael imagined there wasn't a child in the room who had ever heard the song before.

The kids and their adopted grandpa would have stayed in the lodge for the rest of the day, but Michael wanted to let them have one last activity before they boarded the bus for Salt Lake. At the end of Homer's toe-tapping rendition of "Sweet Georgia Brown," he stood and got their attention.

"Everyone, please get your coats, hats and gloves back on. We're ready to head for the tubing hill."

"Tubing?" Kat questioned. "Michael, are you sure about this?"

Michael pulled her to her feet. "I'm sure. I've designed some pretty interesting sleds and tubes, and I've picked a gentle slope designed just for these groups. No one else is allowed on them. I haven't had an injury yet."

"What's after tubing?" she asked, clearly skeptical. "Rocket sleds?"

He laughed. "No. They'll head back to Salt Lake, where they'll have dinner and go to bed. I used to send them to a movie afterward, but their leaders said they were all falling asleep. Tomorrow they'll go to the Hansen Planetarium for a laser show before they fly back to Arizona."

He only wished he could do more.

# # #

Kat stared at her ex-husband, amazed at everything he'd done to make the lives of these children better. The list just seemed to go on and on. She nodded silently, recalling a time the two of them had lain in the green grass and wildflowers on a sunny slope on this very mountain when Michael said, "If I ever become wealthy, I would love to help other people enjoy life. I want to help them do things they couldn't normally do." That was just what he was doing.

He's a good person, Kat reminded herself, a deeply sensitive man who deserves some happiness of his own. She thought again about her plans for pregnancy. She was sure now, more than ever, that Michael would be the perfect father for her child. But was she heartless enough to run away and never let him know about the baby, especially when things were going so well between them? Wasn't this more of a betrayal than ever?

Kat gazed around the room with tear-filled eyes at the children. She would gladly take any one of them for her own, and she knew Michael would do the same. They could both be good parents, just not together.

Or could they do it together?

No. Kat refused to think about that. She couldn't ask Michael to move back; she had promised herself that two years ago. If he wanted to come back, he would. She still didn't know if he wanted that at all. She wanted him to come back because he loved her and no one else, because nothing else would do, because he was ready to commit fully to them and to their relationship. The hurt and disillusionment of his previous neglect still surfaced from time to time; sometimes her self-esteem would plummet once again and it took days before she clawed her way back to the light. Did she want to let herself in for that again?

She broke away from the group and texted Georgi and Tara: I AM SO CONFUSED. WE'VE HAD A GREAT DAY, AND I JUST DON'T THINK I CAN GO THRU WITH THIS.

She was waiting for a response when Michael interrupted with a gentle touch on her elbow. He beckoned, and they led the pack of kids to the tubing hill. Here Kat found he'd created yet another extraordinary experience for the children. Michael had indeed designed a unique set of sleds and tubes complete with seat belts and brakes; some even had steering wheels. The mountain came alive with laughter and squeals of delight and terror.

Jesse talked Kat into taking a turn on a toboggan with him, though she was initially reticent. When they finally came to a stop, the youth leaned the back of his head on Kat's chest and looked up at her. "That wasn't so bad, was it?"

"I guess not," Kat admitted. It had taken her mind off her problems for a bit.

"See? It's fun to try things you're afraid of. Next time it won't be so scary."

Out of the mouth of babes.

It was dusk when the children's bus pulled back up in front of the lodge. The temperature had dropped ten degrees, and leaders and helpers together loaded the kids into their seats. Every youth had a hug for Grandpa Homer and Grandma Celeste. Kat watched as they interacted with her grandfather, her heart full. He had been right; it had been a very rewarding day. She'd never imagined any of it upon waking up.

Jesse was the last to step toward the bus. He'd lagged behind the others, his head bowed, stabbing at a crusty patch of ice with one crutch. Michael and Kat walked over to him.

"Well, Jesse. I guess it's time to go," Michael said.

"I know."

Kat gave him a gentle hug after the boy maneuvered his tired and heavy limbs into a straighter position. "You're a very special young man. Keep in touch, please."

"I will. Thanks for everything."

Michael knelt down in front of the child and took him fiercely in his arms. "I'm going to miss you, son. Promise you'll write or call anytime; the numbers are on that card I gave you. Promise?"

Jesse looked at Michael, and his face was full of sincere honesty. "You're awesome."

Kat felt a tear slip down her cheek. Those words, so simple, were words she would like to tell him herself.

"You're the awesome one, Jesse. You know that, right?"

"I know," Jesse answered with a soft smile.

Michael lifted the child onto the bus, and a few moments later he had disappeared inside.

Katherine and Michael stood for a long, long time after the bus departed. Late afternoon turned to evening and still they stood there, not speaking, not even touching. Each, in their own way, was fulfilled and yet also somehow empty. Worst of all, Kat knew she could never carry out her plan.

Chapter Nine

Celeste invited them over to her condo for dinner. "I could put some spaghetti together in no time," she suggested.

Kat hesitantly turned to Michael. The three of them plus Homer stood in his office. It was one thing to be at home or at this resort with him, but going somewhere else was too much like a date. Not that she missed the irony of that. She had slept with him last night, yet sharing dinner with friends was too intimate?

She was losing her mind. The longer she was near Michael, the more uncomfortable she became deep inside. Her nerves were as scattered as her thoughts. She was wishing for things that could never happen. Michael had never once in the two years since their separation and divorce tried to reconcile. Part of that was surely stubbornness, but wasn't the rest simply desire? He had moved on to a life that didn't include her. Her friends had said he wasn't seriously involved with anyone, but maybe she'd been right to accuse him of his resort being his mistress. Perhaps he'd learned that's all he needed in his life.

Michael surprised her by answering for both of them without consulting her.

"Thanks, Celeste, we appreciate the invitation but I've got something planned. I've been wanting to show Kat this for a long time, and I just called to have it readied. Will you have us some other time?"

"Of course, dear," the older woman said.

Michael reached out and gave Celeste's hand a squeeze; then he shook Homer's. "Thank you for all of your help today. We couldn't have done it without you."

"It was our pleasure. It's a fine thing you're doing here, Kid." Homer patted Michael on the shoulder. "Come on, Celeste, let's go. I just love going home with a pregnant lady."

Homer's statement made everyone stop and stare.

"Homer," Celeste said, bewildered, "I'm not pregnant."

"You're not home yet!"

Celeste and Kat both rolled their eyes and shook their heads. Michael hooted.

"Grandpa," Kat said. "Honestly."

"I've got to remember that line," Michael said, still laughing.

Kat turned away so he couldn't see the blush rise to her cheeks; he could use that line on her tonight and she'd gladly take him up on the offer. No, wait. She wouldn't. She would have before today, but somewhere between breakfast and Jesse R. Staples she had lost her nerve. Her selfish determination had been tempered by the loving concern Michael showed the children. She wasn't certain what she was going to do now.

They walked Homer and Celeste to her car, and as the older pair drove away Michael turned to face Kat. It was snowing lightly, and a flake dropped seductively onto Michael's eyelash like a gentle kiss.

"Now," he said, smiling. "For my surprise."

"Another one?" Kat asked. "You're full of surprises today. What's this now?"

"You just come with me."

They walked toward the stables, and Michael reached down and took her hand. Kat held herself back, but Michael acted totally undisturbed by her standoffish position. It was obvious from his animated step that he was excited.

They moved past Tom and Jerry into a large tack room. There stood a beautiful blond horse tethered to the most exquisite Currier & Ives-type contraption Kat had ever seen. The replica sleigh was bright red, with sprigs of holly hand-painted in minute detail. The sleigh's lines curved and curled around the runners and up to a small black leather seat barely big enough for two. For the tenth time that day, Kat found herself near tears.

"Is this what you had in mind?" Michael asked quietly, standing behind her.

She could only nod. The sleigh had been her idea, something she had always dreamed of owning since the project of Eagle's Nest began. She'd known it would be a popular attraction for couples in love.

"It's perfect," she squeezed out past the lump in her throat.

"Well," Michael said, moving forward. "Climb aboard."

Kat took his outstretched hand and stepped up into the waiting carriage. Michael tucked a sheepskin and wool blanket around her legs then ran to the other side, jumped in and took the reins. After he gave a click of his tongue, the horse moved out through the immense barn doors into the shimmering moonlight.

The sleigh drew much attention as they passed through the busier sections of the resort; admiring smiles and wistful gazes followed them. The lights and sounds eventually slipped away and dimmed behind them, though, and the horse gained speed as they slipped off into the darkness.

The acceleration and the chill of the night air were exhilarating. Kat imagined herself back in time a hundred years earlier, being whisked off to a distant neighbor's ball. She couldn't help but smile openly. The whole atmosphere lent itself to love and laughter, not heartache, despair or somber decision-making that would change the course of her life. She could leave the real world behind her for a little while and just surrender to enjoyment.

"Whoa, Ginger." Michael slowed the horse to a walk. They were entering a thicket of pines, sturdy and ancient.

"Why did you name her Ginger?" Kat asked.

"Just look at those legs. Gorgeous. If ever a horse could dance, it'd be this one."

"She is very beautiful," Kat agreed, admiring the animal.

"So are you."

She felt his eyes on her, and heat rose to her cheeks in spite of the temperature. Blushing? Wasn't she a bit old for such nonsense—and with her ex-husband, no less? She decided to change the subject before she lost any more dignity. "How long have you had her?"

Michael wouldn't let her off the hook. "I've wanted to tell you that all day. With your dark eyes and hair and that white fur hood framing your face…you are as beautiful to me as this entire day has been. And it was a wonderful day."

"You're pretty beautiful yourself, Blake." And hard to resist.

Ginger followed a narrow trail that spiraled up the mountain. Spotlights had been strategically placed in the snow lighting the path without detracting from the magical ambience. The trail grew ever steeper, and suddenly they were in a small clearing. Michael pulled back the reins, and Ginger immediately came to a halt.

Kat gasped. "Oh, my God, Michael. It's incredible."

The view honestly took her breath away. The moon was almost full, and it had risen to light the night with the help of a million stars. White mountains piggybacked each other, ridge after ridge. In the dimness Kat could barely make out the outline of clumps of trees. She felt special yet utterly insignificant at the same time. An ethereal awareness filled her being, and she felt as if she were an infinitesimal part of a much greater plan.

Michael put his arms around her and pulled her near. She could smell the musky, clean scent of him, and it heightened her pleasure in the pureness of the moment. She was surprisingly warm and comfortable with the entire situation. It didn't bother her that Michael held her so closely. It felt…right.

He moved his lips to her forehead and gave her a tender kiss. This special act had been Michael's way of showing adoration since their first date. In fact, a kiss on the forehead was the only kiss he had given her on that first date. It had been perfect then, and it was perfect now. They snuggled in silence, watching the evening sky each with their own thoughts.

Kat became increasingly aware of Michael's body next to hers. Remembering last night, she wanted him to kiss her again. Desperately.

She turned her face to his and smiled. Their cold noses met. He touched an index finger to her cheek and then to her chin, lifting it ever so slightly. Their lips were positioned perfectly, but he didn't kiss her. He searched her eyes and then his lips moved to her forehead again, brushing ever so lightly against her bangs and then down across each cheek and the tip of her nose. Finally, his lips found hers.

For some reason this kiss was different than any that had come before, almost as if it were opening the gate to a new world for them both. Kat shivered with a mixture of the cold night air and the heat of desire. Michael's tongue grazed her teeth, and she opened wider to let him in. His hands were on the small of her back, and he pulled her as close as he could within the confines of the miniature sleigh.

Katherine closed her eyes and let him ravish her mouth. Michael's kiss thrilled her, kept her restless, wanting more. But on this windswept hillside, five feet of snow surrounding them, the chance of going further seemed very remote. Again she was reminded of the few tepid dates she'd had since they split. Would she ever find this kind of intensity with anyone else, or was she doomed to a life of boredom? Worse yet, was she destined to be alone? Maybe that would be better than a life without passion.

He slid the fur hood from her head and pushed the fabric from her throat, moving his mouth slowly to the pulsing spot on the side of her neck, the most sensitive part of her body. There he gently sucked on the pulse, and Kat arched in an age-old pose of submission. He lingered, lovingly, and Katherine felt her soul touch his.

After what seemed like both an eternity and a brief instant all rolled into one, Michael raised his head and spoke in a husky, lust-filled voice.

"I'm hungry."

"Me too," she breathed. And not just for food.

"Good," he said, pulling away. "I've had a splendid picnic prepared for us by my top chef. I'll get it."

Although it was predominately dark on the closed slope, several solar lights were scattered around. Astounded, Katherine watched as Michael jumped from the sleigh and left her panting with desire. By the time he returned, she had regained some of her composure. How he could change gears that quickly was a mystery to her, but he carried two heavy woolen blankets to a flat spot away from the horse and spread them on the crusted snow.

"Make yourself comfortable. I'll be right back."

Kat sat down on the cushiony blankets and pulled her knees up to her chest. A winter picnic…? This had also been her idea. She was surprised that Michael had remembered all the suggestions she had made and had implemented them. It made her feel special— needed, in a way. And she liked knowing that what she thought still counted.

He returned with a wicker basket shaped like a suitcase. Carefully he laid it on the blankets and proceeded to produce an extraordinary scene elegant enough to rival any French restaurant, laying down a small tray and a miniature table with Royal Dolton china and crystal, linen, and ornate silverware with matching candlesticks. After lighting the candles, Michael poured a crisp chardonnay in their goblets and presented the first course from a portable warming oven. The creamy white soup had tiny slivers of carrots and mushroom.

"Tonight, my dear, we will start our feast with a fresh mushroom bisque." He used his most formal voice. "Our second course is endive broccoli salad with warm vinaigrette dressing, after which our main course will be Cornish game hen and stuffing with an orange marmalade sauce, and homemade crescent rolls."

He sounded just like a waiter at Nino's, but the twinkle in his eyes was far more intimate. "And dessert…is a surprise."

Kat's heart fluttered. She was most curious about dessert. She was more than ready for more of his sensual kisses…but when he placed the raspberry crown chocolate torte in front of her, she almost forgot about him.

"This is too beautiful to eat," she exclaimed. The torte had a brownie-type layer covered with glistening raspberry preserves nestled in a cloud of whipped cream. "But, I'll force myself. Please give my best to your chef."

Michael had remembered the combination of raspberry and chocolate was one of her very favorites, but she had never tasted anything quite like this.

"This is absolutely sinful, and I love it."

They munched and chatted and admired the majestic grandeur accompanying their elevation of nearly nine thousand feet.

"Doesn't it seem like we're the last two people on the face of the earth up here?" Katherine asked.

"It does," Michael agreed. "And I'm not trying to wax poetic, but must admit that if I were one of the last two people on the earth, I wouldn't mind the other one being you."

She grinned, amused. "Michael Blake, you are so full of amorous quotes tonight. Have you been reading Browning?"

Michael just looked at her, and there was no smile on his lips. "I'm not trying to fill your head with fantasy, Kat. This is as real as it gets. There's nothing but truth here."

Chapter Ten

Dinner completed and tucked away, Michael gave Ginger a commanding click of his tongue and he and Kat were off once more. Traversing the wintry darkness, Kat sat silently trying to sort through her emotions. For two years now she had made her heart unavailable, and she wasn't at all sure if she could allow herself to open it up again. She'd sworn that she'd never let herself be hurt by Michael again. And yet, he was doing everything right. He'd made her feel tonight like there was no other woman in the world.

"Where are we going now?" she asked. She had assumed they'd be returning to the resort and then her house, but that didn't seem to be the case. They were still traveling upward, heading toward the next ridge.

"I've got one other thing to show you," Michael announced. "Just around the next bend. Are you cold?"

"No, just tired," she lied. She wanted to take him back to her place and make love to him, whether she was ditching her plan or not. He'd spent the entire day increasing her desire, now he was really stringing out the wait.

"Well," Michael said, pulling the reins tighter, "I hope you're not in a *big* hurry. This could take a while."

Great.

As they rounded the last corner, the ridge widened out into a plateau. The area was flat, about an acre of ground covered in large Douglas firs and hundreds of bare quaking aspens. Michael pulled the reins toward his chest, and Ginger turned her head to the left and maneuvered into a small stable that seemed to appear out of nowhere. Michael jumped from the sleigh, unharnessed the horse and quickly brushed her down. It happened so quickly that Kat didn't even speak up. Ginger was soon contentedly munching hay and Michael had returned to Kat's side.

Kat sat motionless. It wasn't hard to put the puzzle together. They obviously weren't going back to the resort for a while, maybe not even tonight. The question then was where they were going. When Michael was a kid he'd loved to build snow caves and sleep in them. She hoped he didn't have something like that in mind.

"Michael?"

He lifted her from the sleigh by her waist and silenced her question with a kiss. "Don't ask me any more questions, Little Miss Impatience. They will all be answered in a matter of minutes."

He led her down a little path, packed snow under their feet and walls made of snow on either side. The trail curled through the trees, and an increasing number of miniature white lights brightened their way. Suddenly, standing serenely in front of them was a new but rustic-looking log cabin. Warmth emanated from the curtained windows. Smoke rose lazily from a tall rock chimney. Kat stared up at the cabin, then at Michael.

"I found those sketches you drew and had an architect work up a blueprint. A designer decorated the inside."

Kat continued to stare at him.

"It was already in the works before we split," he admitted. "Are you ready to go in? I've got to handle one last thing with Ginger. I'll only be a few more moments, but why don't you go in and get warm?"

Kat stopped him with a trembling hand. She had the intense sensation that if she walked through this door she could never go back to where her life had been only yesterday.

Go back to what? she wondered. Independence? No. The last two years had shown her more of what she could do, but Michael had never tried to limit her ambitions. She was more afraid of something else.

A new beginning? A new commitment? Trying to rekindle all that had been right so many years ago, breaking her vow to herself that she'd never trust this man again, at least in terms of his commitment to her?

"Does this place have a bathroom?" she asked.

Michael knew her even better than her friends did. On their wedding night, Kat had stayed in the bathroom for an hour before she dared come out into the bedroom. "You're not nervous, are you?"

"No," she snapped. "I'd just like to powder my nose. Got a problem with that?"

He laughed. "No ma'am. Here's the key."

Kat unlocked the door and pushed it open, and her first sight of the cabin interior made her forget all about her need to hide in the bathroom. The bed was immediately visible. A forest green down comforter with a deep burgundy underside covered it, and lots of fluffy pillows leaned against a delicately hand-carved headboard. That rich antique oak beckoned Kat, and she wandered over to the bed in a dreamlike state and grazed her fingers over it. The green flannel sheets were turned back and had a wispy pattern of snowflakes.

To the left was a nightstand with a tablecloth matching the bed. Very old books rested here, and an oil lantern. To the right of the bed was an exquisite stone fireplace, the hearth carved in the same design as the headboard. A fire was burning merrily within. Several thin candles in brass holders of various heights stood majestically along the ledge. Kat hurried over and lit them.

Above the fireplace hung an oil painting of a sleigh, just like the one they had arrived in, bearing what looked like a couple from the eighteenth-century. They snuggled under a blanket on a deep wintry evening in the forest.

Two comfortable leather chairs stood sentinel on either side of the glowing fireplace, each complete with its own ottoman. The windows on this end of the cabin were long and narrow, and lacy Swedish curtains with a snowflake pattern seemed fitting for the frosty night outside. She could see it had begun to snow, making this whole evening seem even more of a fantasy.

A kitchen was nestled at the other end of the large room. The cupboards were grouped in a U-shape, with a counter at one end. Dark green granite topped the bar. On the other side was a handsome table with two matching chairs. Appropriate. Clearly this cabin was a place for private, intimate moments.

Kat heard her phone beep, and she was surprised that a text would work so far up the mountain. She read Georgi's reply to her earlier message, and her friend was not about to let her quit.

DON'T LOSE HEART WHEN THE PRIZE IS IN SIGHT.

And yet, maybe the prize was Michael and not just a baby.

Knowing Michael might be back at any time, she squelched the urge to tell Georgi her concerns and instead continued to look through the cabin.

Besides the main area, the only other room was the bathroom. Kat walked inside and turned on a light. Even here, the ambience was soft and romantic. The walls were cedar, like in the rest of the house. Thick towels hung from oak racks. The fixtures were antique-looking, clean ivory and brass. The bathtub was an antique like hers at home. An enormous window reached to the floor and invited the secluded woods right in, making the room seem immense.

Michael entered the cabin, walked over and leaned against the frame of the bathroom door. His pleased expression showed he knew she liked the place.

"So, it meets with your satisfaction."

"I'm in *love* with it." She smiled warmly and walked to him. Reaching up, she touched his cheek. "You are an amazing man, Michael."

"I can't take the credit. This cabin was your idea from the beginning."

Kat shook her head. "No, my dear, it wasn't. I remember the conversation vividly. We were discussing the sleigh rides, and I said, 'After their ride, they will go back to the condos.' You said that would be anti-climatic, that a couple needs to have a place of their own, someplace with a bearskin rug in front of a fireplace so they can lie naked in each other's arms and love the winter night away."

"I said that?"

"You did. This was your dream, Michael. But you forgot the bearskin rug. It's not like you to forget an important detail like that," she joked.

Michael walked out to a closet in the main room, turned back with a mischievous grin. "I had forgotten I'd said that, but I must not have forgotten the dream. I had Tim hide it, because I was embarrassed. I thought you'd think it was too…too cliché."

Kat took the rug he produced and spread it out between the two chairs in front of the golden fire. "There is nothing cliché about this, my love. Nor about you."

It was amazing, really. Her own desires were dim in the back of her mind; she wanted nothing more than to fulfill his every fantasy. She just wanted to please him as he had spent the day pleasing her and everyone else.

There was a sweetness to the moment, a languorous reflection and realization that there would be no turning back. Even though they'd had sex the night before, tonight would put them in a different realm entirely. They were both aware of it. They were falling in love all over again, standing face to face, more connected perhaps than they ever had been.

Kat trembled but took Michael's face in her hands. On tiptoes, she brushed his lips with her own. Her entire body burned with the touch.

Michael kept his hands at his sides, and she silently cried out for him to grab her, to press her against his solid chest and crush her in his embrace. After bringing her here, was he having second thoughts? They were on the brink of letting the passion they had so long denied come back into full bloom.

"What is it, Michael?"

He raked a hand through his hair and walked to the window. Shoving his hands fiercely into his back pockets, he spoke without looking at her.

"I'm scared, Kat."

The words and the way he said them broke Kat's heart. She herself had felt this pain.

"What are you afraid of?" she whispered.

"That tonight will be irreversible. That I will never be able to look at you again without wanting you." He turned to face her with anguish in his eyes. "And not just sexually, but emotionally, spiritually...*all* of it. If I can't have you completely, in every aspect of my life, I don't want you at all. I sometimes would have liked to be a modern man who can 'screw 'em and move on to the next adventure,' but I'm not like that, Kat. I'm old-fashioned. I want one woman who will love me completely, passionately, for the rest of my life. Someone I can trust totally."

Kat stood with her arms wrapped around herself. Suddenly she felt cold, very cold. She moved nearer the fire and couldn't look at him. Her eyes were riveted to the flames, and she prayed for the strength and guidance she needed to make the right decision for herself and the child she wanted so dearly...and for Michael. Could she be the person he described? Could he be the person she needed? If she stopped this deception and forgot about having his child before they reconciled, could they maybe just put their relationship back together?

"I need to go to the bathroom."

Kat escaped, and she heard Michael laugh. The mood was broken.

In the bathroom, she looked in the mirror and was startled to see that her face was slightly gray. "You're scared too," she told herself in the glass. She wanted to consult her friends, but she also knew the decision was hers alone. She was the one who would have to live with the consequences.

She paced in the small chamber. This day with Michael had made her see things in an entirely different light. On the slopes she'd decided she wanted a baby desperately but not enough to deceive him. Not now, not after their last few days. Michael would make a great father, and she couldn't go through with it. But was giving up her duplicity also giving up her only shot at getting pregnant? What if things fell through with them as they had two years ago? Funny, she still thought of Michael as the only possible father for her child.

"I'm sorry, baby," she whispered, and laid a gentle hand on her flat belly. "It's not fair to Daddy."

A single tear trickled down her cheek, dropped off her chin and landed on the white fur of her coat collar. When she opened the door she and Michael would start fresh with no hang-ups or secrets—except for the tiny one about trying to seduce him. This wasn't the time or place to tell him that. Someday, when it didn't matter anymore and maybe they had a baby of their own, she would tell him of her silly scheme. She hoped he would laugh.

Kat removed her coat and freshened up. She felt so much better now that she had finalized her decision. The color returned to her cheeks, and she felt blithe, carefree, and just a little giddy. There was so much yet to anticipate.

She returned to the main room, where Michael had put some music on a hidden stereo system and poured two glasses of something transparent and pink. "Did you get everything solved?" he asked, then continued without waiting for an answer. "If you ever become president of the United States, you're going to need ten new bathrooms built into the White House."

She shook her head. "You know, Michael, it must be really inconvenient to know someone as well as you *think* you know me."

"I know you better than anyone else in the world knows you, Kat, and I still love you. Whether that's inconvenient or not, I'll let you say."

He handed her a glass and she took a sip, recognizing the drink as a sparkling water with a hint of strawberry. Surprised, she turned to him.

"No alcohol?"

"Nope. I want every single sense alert for the rest of this night."

Enya serenaded their lovemaking, which was as delicate and powerful as her music. Michael and Kat started slowly, sipping their drinks and talking in soft tones. At last Michael took her glass, and after setting down his own he took her in his arms and swayed them in a gentle glide around the room.

They nestled next into one of the leather chairs. Kat sat on Michael's lap, and he started to kiss her in the way she had craved throughout her life: tender yet passionate, each touch told her in a million ways that she was loved, desired, coveted, hungered and thirsted for. Wave after wave of yearning moved through her, from her toes to her heart and back again. She felt truly fulfilled, and he hadn't even touched her in any intimate places yet!

He trembled beneath her, and instinctively she knew that it wasn't simply from his need. This was an emotional connection, the kind that he had claimed earlier to fear. Kat tried to reassure him with her caresses.

"Michael," she sighed. "I lo…"

The words wouldn't come. She wanted to say she loved him—she *did* love him—but she wanted Michael to say it first.

"What?" he murmured against her ear.

"I said I love…the way you touch me."

They soon migrated to the bearskin rug. Slowly they removed each other's clothing and let the warmth of the fire and each other limn their naked flesh. For an eternity they simply explored each other's bodies, as if this were their first time together. Their connection intensified, and Kat wondered again if they really had a shot. Had they both learned the lessons that were necessary to make a lasting relationship? This lovemaking was one hell of a start.

When Michael stopped them to take precautions, Kat felt none of the last night's annoyance or disappointment. She simply laughed and thought of the condoms she'd thrown away—all for naught. He had a big new box.

"You were pretty sure of yourself, weren't you?"

He smiled sheepishly. "After last night? Hell, yeah."

A sudden thought took her: "Or are you *always* prepared?"

Michael grabbed her ankle and wrapped her leg around his waist. "I was only thinking of you and you know it. I had to go into my own gift shop today and buy these. You should have seen the way Becky looked at me. It was embarrassing!"

"Michael," Kat said, laughing again. "You had the help put this whole evening together for you, right? Someone made the food and someone else came out here and lit the fire?"

"Well, yeah."

"Don't you think they already know what we're doing here?"

"Oh." He chuckled. "I didn't think of that. I couldn't think of anything but you."

He kissed her again, making her weak with desire. She helped him with the condom and then gently pushed him to the floor and positioned herself atop him. Ravishing him with her tongue and lips and breasts, she enjoyed every minute of it. She knew he loved her like this, and she was out to grant him every sexual wish he'd ever had—and one or two he hadn't even thought of yet.

It wasn't long before he was writhing beneath her, and he moved his hands from her breasts to her hips. She watched his eyes glaze over and felt her own do the same. A moment later they released their pent-up anxiety as one.

They held each other for a long time afterward, until the fire burned to glowing embers and they felt a chill come into the room. Michael got to his feet and pulled the comforter off the bed to cover Kat with it. Then he went into the bathroom and returned in a white terrycloth robe, threw a second over Kat, rekindled the fire, and lay down once more.

"Would you like to move to the bed?" he asked gently, his lips in her hair.

"Hmm?" she murmured, almost too sleepy to answer.

He helped her up and guided her to the feather tick mattress. In its warm flannel sheets, Kat purred with contentment. She did the same when he removed his robe and crawled in beside her.

With that warm body curled up behind her, it wasn't long before the loving process started all over again. This time it was her turn to be seduced until she begged for release. Michael started nibbling on the back of her neck, and he worked his lips over the entire length of her body. He teased and tormented her to distraction, and every time she almost reached her zenith, he would pull away and let her ache on top of that peak for a few exquisite moments before he started again. Michael had always been an expert lover, and he reveled in showing her just how masterful he could be. Just before she drifted off to sleep, Kat realized that Michael must have been really caught up in the moment. He hadn't used a condom.

She wasn't really concerned, though. What were the odds, given their situation? And if a life was begun, so be it. Everything else seemed to be happening perfectly, so she would leave the rest to faith.

Her growling stomach woke her sometime later. She slid to the side of the bed and stood, stretching her aching muscles. Then she slipped into the soft robe lying on the floor. Hearing Michael stir, she turned to see him smiling at her with sleepy eyes.

"You're beautiful, Kat."

"And starved. Would you mind going to the sleigh and getting our picnic basket?" She gave him her most alluring smile, imagining the cold night air that one of them would brave. "I'll heat us up some leftovers in the microwave."

He shook his head and pointed lazily to the fridge then turned over as if going back to sleep.

Katherine padded to the kitchen and found a feast in the refrigerator. Delighted, she grabbed a chicken leg and nibbled on it while she cooked some eggs and bacon that she'd also discovered. Looking at her watch, she discovered it was only four in the morning, but she was starving. Making love the way they had was hard work. Putting some bread in the toaster, she set the table and then went to drag Michael out of bed.

"I'm sleepy," he groaned. "Not to mention the fact that I can't walk. Start without me." He pulled a pillow over his head.

Kat yanked it off. "Oh, no you don't. We only have one night in this place, and I plan on making the most of every minute."

"God, Kat. We own the damn place. We could move in here if we felt like it. Let me sleep."

We? She thought she liked the sound of that.

She went over to the table and picked up a piece of bacon, took it back to the bed and passed it in front of Michael's nose. Then, leaning close to his face, she bit into it and hoped the crunch would tempt him.

Quick as a snake, Michael snatched the rest of the bacon from her hand and popped it into his mouth. Then he rose from the bed, moaning, slipped on his robe and limped to the table.

"These robes are luscious," Kat commented, pulling hers tight around her waist.

"They're from the resort. All the rooms have them now."

"Nice touch," she said before biting into a piece of toast.

"Thanks. Your touch is pretty nice, too."

They held hands over the table for a second and then continued their breakfast.

"How about a bath after this?" Michael suggested.

"Sounds heavenly."

Things couldn't have been better. They discussed plans to finish the house in town and then wandered arm in arm to the bathroom. Michael ran the water while Kat brushed her tangled hair. Michael continued their conversation about the renovation.

"How are you going to finish the nursery?"

Kat's brush stopped in mid-air. She didn't answer, but he continued anyway.

"Are you still planning on painting the ceiling like the sky, with a kite border?"

He hadn't forgotten anything.

"Yes, actually, I was."

"Well, I can paint the blue sky, but the rest will be your baby. I'm no artist."

Your baby, she thought. *Well, our baby. Maybe. But all in good time.*

Chapter Eleven

Kat lay across the bed on her stomach and watched Michael clear away the dishes from their second breakfast. They'd made love in the shower last night then fallen back asleep. There'd been a bit more food to cook when they arose, and they'd devoured it hungrily—after they'd made love a fourth time.

She stretched and smiled contentedly at Michael. "This morning was as incredible as last night, Mr. Blake."

Michael shrugged nonchalantly, but the look in his eye was priceless. He had enjoyed himself as much as she had.

There came a knock at the front door, and Michael crossed the room to open it.

"Sorry to bother you, sir," said the young man standing in the snow outside. He was staring down at his boots. "But Rona sent me up here to make sure you hadn't driven Ginger off a cliff or something in the dark last night."

Michael laughed. "That's fine, Tim. We are just getting ready to leave. Everything okay down below?"

Tim nodded, color still high in his cheeks. "It's pretty quiet."

"Okay. Thanks again for checking in. We'll be down in a little while—with Ginger."

"Sure thing, boss. See you later."

Michael grinned at Kat as he shut the door. "Poor kid. I wonder if anyone happened to tell him that you're my wife."

"Ex-wife," she corrected. "That could be even more uncomfortable for him."

Michael pulled her close and pressed his lips to her neck. "It's comfortable for me, and that's all that matters. You make me comfortable."

"Comfortable?" Kat repeated with disgust, remembering briefly how he'd taken her for granted in their previous life. "That is one word a woman never wants to have used to describe her."

"Really?" Michael looked surprised. "Tell me the words that you'd want me to use."

"No. If I told you the words they wouldn't mean anything. You have to come up with them on your own."

A flicker of annoyance crossed his face. "Women. They tell you they want to hear something special, something romantic, then they won't tell you what it is. Are we supposed to be psychic?"

"No," she replied, "you're supposed to be observant. For most of you, that's more difficult than being psychic." She smiled sweetly up at him.

"You need a good spanking," he said.

"Sounds fun," she replied, and went to finish dressing. He slapped her playfully on the rear. Kat forgot all about the past.

They straightened the cabin and promised each other they would return soon, though Michael admitted he'd have to check the register to see when it would be available. "It's very popular. I think it's booked every weekend for the next two months. Besides…" He hesitated until he had her full attention. "It will take me that long to recover from last night."

As they left in the sleigh, Kat looked longingly at the cabin. It had been sunny and bright earlier, but now the sky was overcast, making the day gray and dismal. The snow didn't look white in the muted light, and somehow that depressed her just a little. Kat tried to shake off the melancholy mood. She didn't have a reason to be despondent; she and Michael were together again—a couple. They were starting over, and she thought she could trust their life together would be wonderful from now on. She nestled in to enjoy the ride back to the resort.

"How about 'sexy'?" Michael asked.

"What?"

"Sexy. Is that a word you'd like to describe you?"

"Of course." Kat laughed.

"Okay. What about kind, caring, gentle?"

"I think you're straying from the path. That sounds more like a mother."

"You don't want to be a mother?" Michael asked.

"Not yours."

He thought for a minute and continued. "Witty. Intelligent, sensuous."

"Those work," she encouraged.

"Enthusiastic. Conscientious. Hard-working."

"You're slipping into a letter of recommendation."

"And you're too damn fussy."

"Fussy won't cut it either," she said. Then she grinned.

Michael rolled his eyes. "How about loyal?"

"A dog's loyal."

"That's true," Michael said thoughtfully. "And I don't know too many women who are."

Kat sat up straighter in the sleigh. "I was loyal to you. Even after the divorce."

He looked surprised. "Are you telling me you never slept with anyone after I left?"

"Yes," she said. "I'm telling you exactly that. Never. No one." She'd kissed a few, but that had been it—and more than enough.

"Then where did you learn all those…?" His cheeks actually brightened. "Those new things?"

"I read a lot. I had tons of time."

"You didn't even sleep with that lawyer guy from Salt Lake?"

She shook her head. "He lives with his mother."

"So what?" Michael said. "You have a house of your own, and I know for a fact that he was in Park City with you. Rona said she ran into the two of you at the film festival."

"He came up here once in awhile," she allowed, "but I really didn't go to bed with him. He's thirty-nine, and he lives with his mother."

"Were you afraid she'd call and check up on him if he didn't come home?"

"Michael, you are slow today. I think all that sex depleted the flow of blood to your brain. Listen carefully. When a woman is describing a man, it's the kiss of death when she says he lives with his mother. No other explanation is necessary."

"There must be exceptions to that rule."

"None—unless she's an invalid and he's moved back home to take care of her. Look, when a woman is looking for a life partner, that's just not good material."

"Were you looking for a life partner?"

"Sure," she told him, getting somewhat annoyed. "Weren't you?"

"Hell, no. I thought you only found one of those in your lifetime, and you were mine. I just figured I'd go through the rest of my days trying to find someone like you. I knew I could never do it."

"Oh, Michael," she told him, melting into his shoulder, "sometimes you say exactly the right thing."

His response was a snicker. "The blood must be pumping to my brain again."

As they reached the resort, Kat watched bright swatches of color glide down the ski slopes. A few people sat on the outside decks, and there were two or three groups in hot tubs, but on the whole the atmosphere was quiet and relaxed.

They turned the horse over to Tim, who still averted his gaze when he talked to them.

Rona was the total opposite. The forty-something assistant had no problem with speaking her mind. "It's about time. And I'm surprised you're walking," she said brazenly to Michael. Giving Kat a quick hug she asked, "How did you like the cabin?"

"It's perfect," Kat said, giving Michael a smile. "Absolutely perfect."

"Everything under control here?" Michael asked.

"Yep, no problems. Are you going back to Kat's?"

"Yes, I've got work to do. I've got a contract to complete." He grinned at Kat.

Rona smirked as only an executive secretary could. "You'd better get some rest or you won't be worth a tinker's damn around here next week. And you can't have *two* weeks off."

"Who's in charge here, anyway?" Michael asked, then gave Rona a kiss on the cheek. "Thanks, sweetie, I'll make it up to you somehow."

"I know how. You're good friends with Robert Redford, right?"

"Right...."

"I want a date with him."

Michael laughed. "I'll see what I can do. I'll call you tomorrow."

Rona turned to Kat. "Did he sound very sincere about lining me up with Redford? I don't think he sounded very sincere. Did you?"

Kat grinned. "Since Redford's married, I doubt it."

"I just want a date, I don't want to marry him. Geez, a girl can dream can't she?"

# # #

Michael had a few errands to run, and he also swung Kat by her store to check on a few things, just as she asked; it had been awhile since she'd been in, and she was feeling guilty about leaving her employee Sandra working alone. Everything was fine, however; Sandra had everything well in hand. Still, by the time they got back to the house it was mid-afternoon and there wasn't a lot of time left in the working day. The whole time Kat had been thinking about maybe fitting in another session of lovemaking with Michael. There would be plenty of opportunities to finish the renovations later if they were going to continue their lives together.

As they pulled into the driveway, another car pulled up behind them. Celeste got out and immediately walked over. Kat saw from her expression that the woman was concerned about something.

Kat stepped from Michael's jeep, pulling her collar up around her neck. "Is there something wrong, Celeste?"

"Your grandfather swears he's fine, but last night, he had..." Embarrassed, Celeste tried to reword her sentence. "He overexerted himself."

Michael had gotten out of his jeep, and Kat watched him restrain his laughter. When she reprimanded him with her eyes, he got the hint and went over to talk to Homer whom she saw still sitting in Celeste's car. Their conversation drifted back into hearing.

"How's it going, Homer?"

"Couldn't be better. Celeste is acting like a little mother hen, though. I don't like it."

"She's just concerned about you."

"I had a mother. Been there, done that. Don't need the experience again."

Kat was sure that Celeste heard Homer's annoyance, so she shrugged and motioned to the house. "Why don't we go inside and put on some coffee? Those two can come in when they're ready." She took Celeste by the elbow, and they walked up the icy sidewalk.

Inside, Kat tried to make Celeste feel at ease. She knew last night was a delicate issue, and she really didn't want to discuss it any more than Celeste, but if her grandfather's health was at risk she had to ask some questions no matter how uncomfortable they might be.

After they each had a steaming cup of coffee in front of them, Kat broached the subject. "Tell me what happened, Celeste."

The lovely older woman wrung her hands in her lap. "We were…" She looked up at Kat, helpless embarrassment in her gray eyes.

"I think I understand that part. Just tell me what his symptoms were."

Celeste rushed on with the details, visibly relieved. "Well, his breath seemed to get very labored, and then he almost collapsed next to me. I kept asking if I needed to call a doctor, but he is the most stubborn old mule I've ever met. He wouldn't even let me call *you*."

It was Kat's turn to fight embarrassment. "Celeste," she said, coloring. "I haven't had much to do with this, but don't you think this kind of thing happens quite regularly in a man of Homer's age? I mean"—she thought back to her own experiences of last night and this morning and felt a familiar surge of yearning pass through her—"a much younger man could have those exact same symptoms in similar circumstances."

"Yes, dear, I know that, but it was the way Homer looked…ashen and scared. He did finally admit that he'd never had that happen to him before. When I tried to pursue it, though, he was feeling a little better. He kept telling me it was just because I was the best he'd ever had."

Kat choked on her coffee.

"Sorry, honey," Celeste said. "But you know your grandfather."

"Not as well as you do," Kat muttered under her breath.

After a few moments she decided, "I'm going to give my doctor a call and ask just a few basic questions. Homer won't like it, but that's the way it goes. I also think I'll keep him with me for a few days, just to make sure he's all right. I don't trust him to take care of himself."

"I'll warn you right now," Celeste said, "he's going to balk at staying here. He told me on the way over that he wasn't about to stay with you and ruin your chances of reconciliation with Michael. I'd be glad to invite him back to my house for a few days, though. I'll watch him closely and keep you abreast of any changes. Would that be all right?"

Kat wasn't sure what to say. She really did want more time with Michael, but she also wanted to make sure Homer was okay. But if her grandfather and Celeste were doing what it sounded like… She felt like a mother needing to give ultimatums to a teenager.

Celeste laughed. "I promise we won't do anything that could bring on another attack—if that's what he had."

Kat sighed. "Thank you so much. I'm sure Grandpa would be more comfortable at your house, Celeste. That said, I would like to watch him for the rest of the day and evening. Would you consider staying for dinner?"

The silver-haired beauty grinned. "Only if you let me help prepare it. I love to cook, and I hardly ever get to anymore."

"It's a deal," Kat said. "Now, do you think the guys are still outside? They probably didn't dare come in for fear of what we were discussing." Now that Kat thought of what she'd learned about Homer's leisure activities, she might have stayed outside, herself.

"How are things with you and Michael?" Celeste asked gently, interrupting her thoughts. "If you don't mind me asking. Your grandfather filled me in on a few of the details."

"Things are going very well. I still love him, and I think he loves me."

"Then, my dear, you can work through anything."

The men couldn't have picked a more opportune time to enter. Kat poured them each a cup of coffee.

"Where are the snacks?" Homer asked. "Haven't you got a donut or something?"

"No donuts, Grandpa, but I think I've got some Oreos."

"I guess they'll have to do. Bring me a couple will you, honey?"

Kat handed him a saucer full of cookies then put her hand on his shoulder. "How are you feeling?"

Homer opened an Oreo and skimmed out the frosting with his teeth. Putting the cookie back together, he dunked it in his coffee mug. "I'm just fine," he said between mouthfuls. "My little lady here is a worry wart. That's all."

Kat set her mug in the sink and motioned for Michael to follow her into the front room.

As soon as they were through the door, Michael took her in his arms. "I haven't had a kiss for an hour. I'm going into withdrawal."

He kissed her with pleasing abandonment, but Kat pulled away after a few moments of pleasure. She wanted to let him know what was happening. "Michael, I'm worried about Homer. I think I'm going to call my doctor and make sure that we're not missing warning signs."

"Homer's fine, Kat. Good Lord, he's eighty-six years old. How many men do you think are still sexually active at that age? So he breathes a little heavy and has to rest after, so what? I do the same thing!"

"I know," Kat said, preoccupied. "I thought of that."

"Did you now?"

She turned and smiled at him. "Yes. I did."

"Already looking for my shortcomings, are you?"

"No, dear. I didn't say you were short. At all."

"Cute. Very cute."

She shook her head and sighed. "I'm going to go upstairs to call the doctor so that Homer won't hear. He'll have a fit if he thinks we're babying him. Oh, and by the way he and Celeste will be staying to dinner. Is that okay with you?"

"It's your house," he said with a shrug.

Our house, Kat wanted to say, but she knew it was too soon for that. Michael did seem pleased, however, that she had included him in the decision.

"I guess I'd better get my butt in gear and get something done," he said, smiling. "I have a real taskmistress for a boss."

A few minutes later she'd made her call—unsuccessfully. Heading back downstairs, she passed Michael in the hall. The attic corridor was narrow, and he took full advantage. Hands full of tools and paintbrushes, he crowded close. Their chests touched, and his lips puckered up like a child waiting for a kiss. Kat just kissed him and shook her head at his silliness.

"Did you talk to the doctor?" he asked.

"No, she was with a patient. Her receptionist said she'd have her call me before she leaves for the evening."

"Ah. Are you going to help me up here?" His eyes were hopeful, and she could just imagine the fun they might have. But not with Celeste and Homer downstairs.

"No, I'm going to fix dinner."

He grinned and shrugged, though she could see he was a bit disappointed. "Okay, I'm starved. If you're going to work me as hard as you have the last three days, you're definitely going to have to keep fuel in the tank."

She definitely intended to keep him working. "How does a juicy steak and baked potato sound?"

"Perfect. Call me when it's ready."

"It will be an hour or so. I'll put the potatoes in the oven and do a bit of sous-chef work, then I've got to run to the store to get some steaks. I think I'll get Homer and Celeste to go, too. They're parked behind me. We won't be long."

She knew that she didn't want to be away from him very long. The last two years had been long enough.

#

Michael finished puttying the nail holes in the extra bedroom and went into the nursery. There he opened a can of blue paint the color of the sky on a soft summer day, just the hue of which made him happy. Maybe someday a child of his would wake up to this blue sky. It was the first time in a very long while that he had dared to hope for such a thing.

As he stirred the paint, Michael thought of how rapidly his life had changed. A few short days ago he was a successful but lonely businessman with lots of acquaintances, a few close friends and an ex-wife. His greatest excitement was buying a new property in Switzerland and beginning the process of building another resort. Now, for the first time in ages he was excited about the personal possibilities that might be opening up. But he couldn't get too excited too quickly. At least, he had to be aware of the problems they faced so he and Katherine could overcome them. Their reconciliation seemed complete, but there were always bumps in the road. There was rebuilding yet to do.

Michael poured some paint into a sloped pan and pressed a roller up and down until it was covered in blue. Then he climbed the ladder and started to roll the ceiling, thankful that the task didn't take much brainpower. It would give him plenty of time to consider his future.

He loved Kat. He really did, and the past few days had been almost perfect. Despite that, he didn't trust her—or himself for that matter. Not fully, which was what marriage was all about. Last time it had failed. Trust would have to come back to them gradually, for time was the only sure healer of the pain they had experienced, the only proof of unwavering commitment. Trust came from honesty and communication. He needed a bit more time to work through his feelings, but he was confident they could work through them together.

He'd just stepped from the ladder to refill his roller when the phone rang. Roller in hand, he went to answer, not knowing if he were the only one left in the house. Picking up the receiver, he was just about to say hello when he heard Kat say it first.

Another voice followed. "Katherine, this is Barbara Noble."

"Hi, Doctor."

Michael decided to stay on the line and hear what the physician had to say about Homer's condition. He had thought a little more about what had happened, and perhaps he was being just a little too flippant about the whole thing. After all, Homer *was* getting up there in age. Both he and Kat loved the old man dearly. They wanted to keep him around for as long as possible.

Kat explained the situation, and the doctor assured her that her grandfather was probably fine, but she also cautioned Kat to watch him carefully for any other signs of overexertion or extreme fatigue. She also suggested looking out for a swelling of the feet or ankles.

"This could be the beginning of congestive heart failure," the doctor admitted.

Michael was suddenly worried. Downstairs he knew Katherine would be beside herself.

The G.P. continued: "I know that sounds terrible, but even if it is congestive heart failure, it can be controlled with medication if handled properly. So don't worry yourself sick. Actually, why don't you bring him in tomorrow at two and we'll check him over thoroughly?"

"Okay, I'll see you at two. Thank you, Barbara."

"Oh," the doctor said, just before any of them hung up. "Katherine. While I've got you on the phone, how are your plans coming? Are you pregnant yet?"

"No, not yet," Kat said with a glib little laugh. "But I'm not worried about it anymore. I know it will happen sooner or later. Everything's falling into place."

"Great," the doctor replied. "Keep up the positive attitude. It seems to help in situations like yours. See you tomorrow."

Michael stared down at the phone in his hand as if it had just delivered a warrant for his death. The receiver burned his flesh and yet he couldn't let go. He noticed a few specks of blue paint on it, and somewhere in the back of his mind he wondered if Kat would be angry.

Pregnant? *Plans?*

It all fell into place. The auction, the way she'd behaved that first day… Kat hadn't brought him here to finish her house. She had tricked him into staying here so that she could get pregnant. And he had fallen for it, hook, line, and sinker. How could he have been so damn stupid! What had she planned on doing after she conceived, though? Would she kick him out again—or hadn't she even planned on telling him? What the hell was he to her, just some kind of machine, a stud hired for four thousand dollars to come in and *service* her?

From some unknown place inside his gut Michael felt a heat build until it threatened to consume him. The last of his strength and will sapped away, and he sat down hard. As if in slow motion, the roller slipped out of his hand and dropped to the floor, spattering sky-blue paint across the hardwood floor.

Chapter Twelve

Kat hummed along with her favorite jazz singer, Diana Krall, as she tossed a green salad. Steaks sizzled with a tangy aroma, and the tantalizing smell of baking lemon bars gave the kitchen a fresh scent of spring. Celeste was setting the dining table for four, using Kat's best china and linen napkins. Fresh rolls sat in a covered basket, and candles were ready to be lit as soon as the steaks were finished. Homer was in the living room watching the six o'clock news.

Kat poured a glass of wine for herself and one for Michael. She removed her apron, took one long-stemmed goblet in each hand and mounted the stairs, but she stopped dead in her tracks at the top when she saw the mess. A burst of blue paint was spattered across the hardwood floor.

"What happened?" she exclaimed.

Michael was in the hall instantly. High-strung, agitated.

"What the hell does it look like? I had an accident with the roller, but don't you worry your pretty head about it. You paid four thousand dollars for this little project, and by God you'll get your money's worth."

Kat almost dropped the wine glasses. On shaky legs, she walked into the nursery and set them on the window seat. "Michael, what's the matter?"

"What do you think is the matter? I dropped the damn roller. Does there have to be something wrong more than that?"

"No," she said cautiously. "But don't worry about the hall, I'll help you clean it up. And then we'll have dinner. I'm sure you'll feel better after you get something in your stomach."

"I'm not hungry," he snapped.

"You were starving an hour ago."

"Well, that was an hour ago," he threw back.

She just stood staring at him.

"Look. I'm not coming down to dinner. I'm not hungry, and I don't want your help. Any questions?" He walked away before she could reply.

Kat sat down on the rough wood of the window seat in a puzzled stupor. Michael was obviously greatly disturbed about something. What had happened? She sat there until she heard Celeste at the bottom of the stairs calling her name.

"Kat, dear? I'm afraid the steaks are quite well done, and the lemon bars are a touch too crispy."

"I'll be right down."

Kat tried to salvage the burnt meal. The steaks were edible, but she threw the lemon bars in the trash, pan and all. She lit the candles for Celeste and Homer and put their food in front of them, but her mind was racing.

"I'm sorry about this," she said. "Now, if you'll excuse me for a minute, I'm going to take Michael's food up to him."

The older couple looked at her with curiosity.

"He's right in the middle of a project, and he doesn't want to clean up to eat," she lied. "I'll be back in a minute." She was actually afraid to go back upstairs, but she had to see if he was still as upset as he had been a few minutes earlier.

When she reached the attic, this time she found him sitting cross-legged in the middle of the nursery with his head in his hands. Something was terribly wrong, and she had no idea what it could be. Her heart went out to him, and she stood in the doorway with his dinner, letting it get cold, not knowing what to say.

She shifted positions, and a creaking floorboard squeaked under her foot. Michael was instantly on his feet, picking up a paintbrush. He glanced in her direction.

"I told you, I don't want anything to eat."

"I know, but I thought you might get hungry in a while. I'll just leave this here on the window seat." She then tried to lighten his mood. "I think that color's going to work nicely," she said, looking at the ceiling that he'd already painted. "If it's dry by morning I'll start on the clouds."

She waited for a comment. When she didn't get one she asked, "Will that be all right?"

"You're the boss. Whatever Katherine wants, she finds a way of getting."

"Where did that come from?" She was getting just a little sick of his attitude. When Michael didn't speak, she muttered, "I'm going back downstairs and leave you to your own miserable company."

"Suits me. Better than the other options I have at the present time."

She couldn't stand to let him have the last word. With his previous statements he had lost any sympathy she'd had for whatever happened, and now she was burning with fury and sadness. "When you're ready to tell me what's bugging you, I'll be downstairs."

She descended the steps with her head held high, but as soon as she was on the bottom stair the erectness left her and she crumbled into a heap. Homer was instantly by her side.

"What's wrong, honey?"

Kat felt silly. "Nothing, Grandpa, I'm fine. I must have slipped on something." Boy, she was getting good at inventing stories. She was disgusted with herself.

"Come and eat your supper."

"I'm not hungry." At least that statement was very true. Katherine felt nauseated from fear and rejection. What in the hell was going on? What could have possibly happened to make Michael so angry and morose?

"What's the project the Kid's so engrossed in?" her grandfather asked.

"Himself," she said bitterly, before she could stop herself. She regretted it the minute the reply escaped her lips.

Homer was quiet for a moment, letting that sink in. Celeste quietly rose from her chair and stepped into the living room, clearly trying to give them some privacy. Kat, still sitting on the bottom stair, put her head in her hands.

"Want to talk about it?" asked her grandfather, coming to sit on the stair next to her.

"I would if I had a clue as to what to tell you, but I don't. I honestly do not know what's wrong. Everything was perfect one minute, and the next everything was wrong." She shook her head. "I can't imagine what could have happened."

"Would you like me to have a little man-to-man with him?"

"No, Grandpa. But thanks anyway. Michael's too damn stubborn to talk to anyone civilly right now. I've *never* seen him like this, even when we split up." She remembered those days like they were yesterday. Was it all happening again?

Kat got up and busied herself with Celeste and Homer's dishes. She couldn't bear to think that she might be losing Michael again, not after the past two days. Not after she'd worked past her fear of trusting him. Fate wouldn't be so cruel as to let her taste sweetness for three days and then jerk it away. It just couldn't.

She took one load then left the rest of the dishes where they were and went to change her clothes. After changing into some grubbies she'd clean up the spilled paint. Her relationship with

Michael was worth fighting for, and at least this way she'd be working near him. Maybe, just maybe, he would open up to her.

When she returned from changing, Celeste was sitting alone in the main room reading *Reader's Digest*. It was an issue featuring stories on medical issues, and Kat realized guiltily that she'd almost forgotten about her grandpa's condition for the last hour or more. Possibly congestive heart failure the doctor had said?

"Where's Homer?" she asked Celeste.

"I think he's upstairs with Michael."

"Oh no." She didn't know what her grandpa would say, but she doubted it would be very helpful. Bad jokes weren't likely to pull Michael out of his bad mood.

"Kat, let Homer talk to him. Sometimes it really does help to confide in someone of your own gender."

"I know," Kat admitted. "It's just that…Michael's in such a foul mood I'm afraid he might upset Grandpa." That was true, actually. "By the way, I made an appointment for him to see my doctor tomorrow at two. If you would like to go with us for moral support, I'd love to have you."

"I'll be happy to," Celeste agreed.

There was a moment of silence. Kat finally shook her head and said, "I'm going upstairs to do some cleaning. I hope you don't mind. I know I'm being a terrible hostess tonight."

"Don't even think about it," Celeste said, dismissing the whole affair. "I feel like we're family, and you don't have to entertain family."

Kat gave the woman a hug. "Thanks. You're a darling." Then she went to the kitchen to fortify her courage with a glass of water.

She met her grandfather there. He looked very tired, and his brow was drawn in a serious line. Before she could speak, he took her by the shoulders and looked directly into her eyes. Kat felt him shaking, and she knew he was upset as he'd been in a long while.

"I don't know what's happened to that boy, but I'm here to tell you that you'd better get to the bottom of it, and fast. That kid is hurting something awful, and it has to do with you. Young lady, if you let this go and it festers and swells, you might lose him once and for all. If you're half the woman I think you are, you won't let the best thing that ever happened to you walk out of your life."

"But Grandpa, I—"

He cut off her rebuttal. "Don't be whining to me. Get your butt up those stairs and work this out with him. Michael's made some mistakes, but so have you. So, big deal. Everybody screws up sometimes. There's nothing here you can't fix if you try hard enough."

Kat wanted to believe that was true. She just didn't know what to fix.

She climbed the stairs once more. The paint had already dried, so she picked up a putty knife and got down on her hands and knees to scrape. She could hear Michael in the nursery pounding nails into wood. Oh, how she wished he would start whistling again and this last hour would just disappear. Why wouldn't he open up to her and tell her what was bothering him?

She shook her head in dismay. Michael could be so damn stubborn sometimes. And his way of dealing with things was to simply clam up and work through anger or depression on his own. Or he let it fester until neither of them could handle it.

Kat always wanted to scream until she felt better, but Michael usually refused to fight with her.

"Don't do that."

His voice startled her, and its harshness made Kat jump. He was standing in the doorway with a look of combined disgust and sadness.

"The longer it stays, the harder it'll be to get off."

He turned his back on her. "I'll do it. Just leave it."

"This is my house, Michael. If I want to get this off the floor before it ruins the hardwood, I will."

He turned around, his eyes cold. "You're right. This is your house. You do what you damn well please." He retreated once more into the nursery.

Kat couldn't believe what she was hearing. She sat on her knees, the hard floor sending searing pain up the front of her thighs. Swallowing bile she tried to compose herself, but that wasn't going to happen. So she finally gathered her wits and courage and yelled, "What in the hell happened?"

She got up off shaky knees and threw down the putty knife. It skidded across the floor and hit a mopboard with a metallic-sounding thud; then she strutted into the nursery and moved into his space, her face only inches from his.

"You came up here an hour ago and everything was fine. Better than fine!" Each word got a little louder than the one before. "I don't know where this peevish attitude has come from, but I demand to know what changed."

It was Michael's turn to raise his voice. "Demand? Demand! How dare you? You bought my services for a week and that's what you got, but you don't own me. I'm not some piece of meat that you can chew up and spit out."

His eyes were narrow chips of black ice. That intensity made Kat step back, but it didn't diminish her fury. "What are you talking about? I thought we got through all that. If that's how you feel, what was last night all about? Just sex? You were *so* desperate to get laid that you planned that whole amazing night? That's pathetic."

She knew she was taking the wrong approach, but she couldn't seem to stop herself. This was a problem with which she'd always struggled. When she became this agitated, she tended to repeat herself. She also tended to go on the offensive.

Michael walked slowly toward her. His words came out short, clipped. "In all the years we've been together I thought I knew you, but I suddenly came to the realization that I don't. I don't know who the hell you are, or what you even stand for."

He sighed. His anger was rapidly changing to resignation, and that terrified Kat. If he got again to the point of acceptance, she would lose him forever. She didn't want that. She had to do something, but she had no idea what could be done. What could possibly have set him off?

Michael moved to the window and stared out. Night had fallen, and the sky was black. He obviously wasn't going to tell her what had changed his mind. Not now at least.

An enormous crash came from the other end of the hall, jerking Kat and Michael to life.

"What was that?" Kat said.

Michael just swore under his breath.

Kat heard another sound, this one faint and blood-chilling. It was a weak male voice. Homer.

Both Katherine and Michael ran to where they had heard the clatter. Now the silence was more startling than any noise. The attic door was ajar, and Kat raced up the steep, narrow stairs of the third floor with Michael right behind. One dim light swayed in the rafters, making a shadowy ghost of a silhouette slip back and forth across the room.

Kat noticed some boxes overturned, papers and books spilling out, but she couldn't see Homer. She moved to the boxes, and Michael did too. He picked up one.

"Homer?" Michael called in a hushed voice.

"Grandpa?" Katherine's voice was full of tears.

Then they heard it, the resonant slam of the door at the bottom of the stairs, the scratching of the metal latch being slid into a locking position. Homer's reedy voice crept up the stairs in a muffled but miffed tone, "I'm fine, but you two aren't. And I'm not letting you out of there until you've settled your differences. Celeste and I will be back in the morning. Have a good night, kids."

Trapped together? Kat didn't dare look at Michael. She slumped onto the floor in a pile of papers.

Michael just said one word. "Damn."

Katherine realized what surrounded her, what had spilled out in a mess of documents, soiled and scattered. Her life. Their life together. A marriage license, ticket stubs, ski passes, love letters, pictures… Hundreds of pictures.

Her grandfather had seen to everything. Kat knew for a fact that these boxes had recently been stored at the very back of the attic, under the eaves. She had placed them there on purpose so that they would be very hard to get to, and she was so afraid of spiders that she'd figured she would never venture upon them again. Now, thanks to Homer, they had stepped from the shadows.

Chapter Thirteen

Michael wandered over to a scarred rocking chair and lifted an enormous pink teddy bear from the seat. He plopped down wearily and held the bear on his lap. He had won the bear for Kat at the state fair in the first year they were married. That night he had told her they would save it for their first child. He wondered now, bitterly, if she was indeed carrying his first child.

Across the attic, she was hunched over and silent. Michael stared at her bent dark head and puzzled over what had happened to her integrity. She was breathing heavily, and that made him think of last night. She was still gorgeous and as alluring as ever, and he was completely disgusted with himself for still desiring her sexually, even after he knew how she had tricked him. He could never trust her again, and he needed to get that through his big thick head.

He wanted to shake her until she explained. Somehow, somewhere, there had to be a reasonable excuse for all of this. But he knew there wasn't. He'd heard the doctor with his own ears, once on the phone and a thousand times since in his memory.

How are your own plans coming along? Are you pregnant yet? Michael clenched the teddy bear tighter to his own aching belly.

Kat picked up something that looked like a photograph. A moment later she started reaching around herself and gathering things up, throwing handfuls of papers and photos back into the box while muttering incoherently to herself. Michael stopped watching. Her pain was almost as obvious as his own.

He got up and walked down the stairs, pushed hard on the door. It didn't budge. He and Kat were locked in all right, and they weren't going anywhere until Homer came to let them out. This lock had been taken from an old mining shaft, and it could keep a hundred ponies penned up. Antique locks were getting harder to come by as the years progressed, and he and Kat had decided together to use the ornate clasp. Now he wished Kat had never purchased the damn thing.

He trudged back to the loft. "Your grandpa's a crazy old coot," he snapped. His words were impudent but his tone held little conviction. Then he glanced down and saw what Kat had in her lap, what she was desperately trying to hide.

Leaning down on his haunches, Michael reached for the photo album. It was leather bound, and he knew before he opened it that he shouldn't. Emotion clouded his eyes as he stared down at the first page. It was a baby picture of him: fat, a square little body, white hair, eyes too big for his face. He stared down at the little boy and wondered what his own child would look like. Would he ever even get to see one? What *had* she planned to do? How had she planned to get away with this?

God, he wanted to choke her until she told him every detail. Homer had been right. Maybe he should just get it all out in the open and let her explain; let her justify her sordid little tale of deception. But he was afraid. He didn't want to hear from her own lips that she had been so selfish and dishonest. For some unknown reason, even to himself, Michael didn't want Katherine to be any less thoughtful and kind than what he already believed; he didn't want her to change from the woman he had married and loved for such a long time. He wanted to have a reason to forgive her, to find that there had been a gross misunderstanding. But there was none, and begging wouldn't make one exist.

He slammed the book shut and threw it on a pile. "Well, this will be as good a night as any to go through all this junk and make three piles—yours, mine, and the junkyard's. Throw everything at the bottom of the stairs that neither of us wants. Then, when Homer gets back, which better be soon, we'll have accomplished something."

"I don't think that's what Grandpa had in mind," Kat said.

Michael just ignored her.

They worked in silence for several minutes. Finally Michael heard Kat muttering, "Yours, mine, the junkyard's." She was repeating it like a mantra.

"Is this baseball mitt any good?" she asked, holding up a glove and throwing it to him.

He eyed it for a minute. "It would be good for a kid." He doubled up his fist and pounded it. He and Kat locked eyes for a second, but neither of them spoke. Michael finally averted his gaze. "Maybe we better make a fourth pile, for the Salvation Army."

"What about this old teddy bear?" he asked after a moment. He carefully watched Kat's response, knowing that she wouldn't actually come out and say, "I'm keeping that for my baby," but surely her expression would give something away.

She glared at the pink bear. "Give it away. I won't be needing it."

Michael was startled by the response. He watched her face to see if she was lying, but he knew Kat well enough to see that she wasn't. Maybe she didn't want the toy because he had given it to her… But even as he considered that, he knew there was more to it. There were a couple of puzzle pieces missing here, and he wasn't sure how to go about locating them.

She had seemed so sincere about making their relationship work. That really bothered him when he remembered. Perhaps she had seduced him with the purpose of getting pregnant; then when he seemed susceptible to the idea she decided to string him along for some extra cash? No, that wasn't like her at all. But, then, what the hell did he know? Having a child and not telling the father wasn't her style either, but she had perhaps planned that, so why not the rest?

"Make sure you take these duck decoys," Kat spoke up curtly. "I step over the damn things every time I come up here for something."

"Throw them over here," he grunted.

"I'm not picking up the slimy things."

"They're not slimy. They're made of rubber. Quit being such a baby." But that was a bad choice of words, he thought.

"They haven't been cleaned since the last time you used them. They've got mold growing on them. And I'm not the baby. You are."

"Mold doesn't keep growing for seven years, and speaking of babies...there's a box of tiny clothes over here. Where did they come from?" Michael held up a blue sleeper with a train on the lapel. Again, he watched Kat closely. Even with the indistinct lighting, Michael could see that she blanched.

"Georgi gave them to me after she had her last baby." Her voice was a shaky whisper.

"Where do you want me to put them?"

She walked slowly over and took the pajamas from his hand. Touching the fabric to her cheek, she quietly and meticulously folded the outfit and set it back in the box. "Put them in the giveaway pile, please. Put the whole box there."

Damn, but she confused him. Michael couldn't figure out her reaction. Why was she giving away all her baby paraphernalia? Unless... She had told the doctor that she wasn't pregnant yet, and now she likely guessed he was leaving her for good. Maybe she didn't think she had a chance of getting that way unless it was him.

He couldn't believe it. Kat was a successful, beautiful woman. She could have her choice of men. And she had enough money to have a baby in a hundred different, modern ways, without having a man truly involved at all. Why was she so fixated on him? Worse,

Michael was beginning to feel sorry for her. What was wrong with him? How could he possibly have sympathy for a woman who planned to use him for a stud service without his permission?

The room was starting to look cleaner. There were three distinct piles on the floor, and the path leading to the stairs was covered with trash. The only thing left to do was divide some furniture that had been sitting around since the first time they split.

"I can't believe two whole years got away from us before we got to this mess. I thought about coming over and cleaning it out once in awhile, but something more important always came up." Michael wouldn't let himself believe that his reason for leaving his stuff in the house could have a deeper and more disturbing meaning. "Whose old rocker was this?" he asked. "I've forgotten."

"My grandma's."

"Okay." He lifted it from a corner and set it near Kat's pile. "Wasn't that brass headboard over there my grandparents'?"

Kat nodded. "You'll have to have some work done on it, but it can be restored beautifully."

Michael moved two or three things out of his way to get to the head- and footboards. He stopped dead in his tracks halfway there, his heart stopping in his chest.

"What is it?" Kat asked. "It's not a black widow is it?"

"Huh?" Her question brought Michael back to his senses.

"The spider," she prompted.

Michael looked down at what had given his heart such a lurch and shook his head. "No spider. I thought I saw a mouse." He knew how frightened she was of spiders, and they had seen some huge ones up here in the past. He knew his lie would put her at ease. She wasn't at all afraid of mice. He was.

She got up and came toward him, laughing lightly. "Mice are cute, Michael. Haven't you seen the movie *Cinderella*?"

Michael didn't want her coming any closer; he didn't want her seeing what stood behind an old chest of drawers, didn't want to deal with the emotions that were washing over him like a deluge. He tried to match her banter. "Haven't you seen…*Charlotte's Web?*"

"Yes, I saw it and I read the book, but I covered my eyes every time Charlotte was on the screen and I put tape over her on the book."

She pushed past him to deal with the mouse and saw it. Nestled in the corner of the attic was what he'd been trying to hide: a cradle. It was the cradle she'd purchased from an antique dealer for her shop but could never part with, and when she saw it Kat dropped to her knees. Michael watched her collapse, remembering all the times she'd laughed about them having a child together sometime in the future. It had never happened, and now it likely never would.

He wanted to go to her, but he couldn't. No, he *shouldn't*. It wasn't his place. It would only confuse her. Besides, she didn't deserve to be comforted. This was all her devious plan, and it had backfired.

Kat raised a quivering hand and ran her fingers along the oak, leaving a trail of fine wood exposed beneath the dust. Michael studied her, watched as a single silent tear slipped down her cheek, her chin, and finally fell onto the cradle, leaving another clean spot.

He couldn't stand it. Instantly his hands were on her forearms, this time with strength but no resentment. He pulled her to her feet and drew her to his chest. He didn't want to do this, but he couldn't help himself. He'd known she wanted a baby someday; they had dreamed about starting a family together when the time was right. He'd just had no sense that she might become so desperate that she would stoop to such preposterous ways of getting one.

"Kat, listen to me." He tried to sound fatherly, but his passion flared again when he smelled the fragrance of her hair. He fought it back. "I know you wanted a child, but you're still young enough to get pregnant. Many people aren't starting their families until their mid-forties. Don't worry, you'll meet someone who will give you everything you need someday, and it will be worth the wait."

There. He had done his duty. He stepped away, not looking to see her expression. Now he needed to put as much distance as he could between them.

He looked at his watch and sighed. Midnight. He was afraid that Homer really wasn't coming back tonight. And he was starved. What he wouldn't give for that plate of burnt steak and potato. He began to pace.

"I'm hungry," he confessed after a few moments and he could stand it no more. "Is there anything up here to eat?"

Kat had been standing quietly in the corner. "I had a case of pineapple stored up here somewhere, but we don't have a can opener."

"You find the pineapple and I'll get it opened. I found a pocketknife in my hunting vest."

Kat grimaced. "I'm not eating anything you open with that filthy knife. You've cleaned dead things with that."

"No kidding. It's easier than cleaning live animals with it." Michael spit on the blade and wiped it on his jeans. "It's clean, see?"

Kat gave him a disgusted look, then walked over and found the case of pineapple.

"So don't have any," he said lightly, taking the can she offered. "I can eat the whole thing myself."

Within a few seconds he had pried one end loose and was delightedly slurping juice. He speared one of the chunks and passed the knife in front of Kat's nose. He could tell she was hungry, and after the third pass she whisked the piece from the tip of the knife and put it in her mouth.

Michael grabbed another can of pineapple and two old Beanbag chairs with duct tape plastered all over them to keep the Styrofoam beads inside. "Why didn't we ever throw these stupid things away?"

"Because," Kat told him. "We made love for the first time in one of them and swore we'd never get rid of them." She blushed when she said it, but her eyes held a challenge.

Michael started to laugh. "God, we were young and silly, weren't we?"

"Not so silly."

"Well," he decided, popping another chunk of fruit into his mouth. "Right now, I'm sure glad we didn't throw them away."

Kat shrugged. "There's a stack of games on the top shelf over there that you need to go through. I don't want any of them for myself, but they're all in good shape. I thought you could take them to the resort for your kids to play when they're not on the slopes."

Your kids. Michael wasn't sure how to respond to that.

Kat started through the pile, lifting the boxes one by one. "Oh wow. Here's Mystery Date."

"Never heard of it."

"That's because it's just for girls. I remember one time I went home from college for a weekend and my mother was cleaning out the basement. She was going to throw this away and so I took it back with me. Tara, Georgi and I played it for hours and giggled and laughed until our sorority mother told us to shut up." She paused a moment then turned. "It's only twelve-thirty, and I'm not tired. We're likely stuck here all night. Wanna play?"

Michael raised an eyebrow. "Play what?"

"Mystery Date."

Michael snorted. "You're kidding, right? I'll have you a game of Monopoly."

"No way, Mr. Entrepreneur. Playing Monopoly with you is like playing Trivial Pursuit with Einstein. What about Life?"

"What about life?"

"The game, Michael. We're both on equal ground there. We've both screwed up ours."

"Speak for yourself," he retorted. "I happen to be a very wealthy man."

"There's more to life than money," she said.

"My, my, this stuffy air is making you exceptionally wise tonight, Katherine."

She grabbed the game and set it up between their two beanbags. He grumbled a bit, but it didn't seem like there was a heck of a lot else to do.

"Okay, spin to see who's first," Kat said.

"I should be first. I don't want to play the stupid game."

"Just spin the dial."

"Yeah, yeah. Okay." Michael looked around. "I'm getting cold, though. Did you see any blankets while you were cleaning?"

"Just one." Kat walked over to a microwave box and pulled out a quilt. From a nail in the corner she produced a ratty green army jacket. "I'll take the quilt. Here's a coat for you."

Michael grimaced. "Gee, thanks, darlin'. That's swell of ya."

Kat gave him a pointed smile. "What did you spin?" she asked, returning to her seat.

"A ten."

"Oh, sure," she said.

"Well, I did. I'm first. How much money do we get to start?"

"Two thousand dollars and a car."

"Two thousand dollars. How old is this game? You paid more than that for a week of work and sex." He hadn't been able to help himself, and his barb hit home.

"Spin," she commanded through clenched teeth.

"'Find circus elephant! Collect $1,500 reward.'" Hm. Maybe this game would turn out okay.

Kat took her first turn. "'Meet future spouse! Pay $500 for diamond ring.'"

"I guess your next husband will get off easier than your last."

"Just play the damn game," Kat growled.

Michael spun another ten. With a smirk he moved his plastic car forward. "'Tornado blows you back to start'?"

Kat laughed. "That's what you get for being such a smartass. My turn." She read the square to herself and frowned.

"Not fair, Kat. You have to read them out loud."

"'Get married. Add spouse. Collect gifts.'"

"Great! I like this game. Now that you're married again I'm finally off the hook. Maybe he'll fix up this place and—"

"You better be careful. There might be another tornado in your future."

Michael hurried up and spun. "'Eccentric Aunt leaves 100 cats. Pay ten thousand dollars to give them away.' It should say eccentric grandfather locks you in attic with ex-wife. I don't have ten thousand dollars, so I guess I lose."

"Not so fast," Kat said. "You'll have to borrow some money from the bank."

Michael stared at her and shook his head. "Who invented this game? It's too real. It's like playing Let's Go to the Dentist."

They continued playing. Michael was priding himself on having a sarcastic comeback for every square Kat landed on, and then he landed on something that sobered him considerably.

"Read it out loud, Mr. Blake. It was your rule, remember?"

"'Add baby daughter. Collect presents.'"

# # #

Kat bit the inside of her cheek. *Add baby daughter.* Michael had been right; this was like going to the dentist. Of course, the whole night had been like going to the dentist. One thing after another had made her want to cry.

There had been that picture of Michael and her cutting their wedding cake. One of her in her wedding dress, with Tara and Georgi wearing lacy collars and floppy hats. She missed her friends tonight; she could use some sound advice. Another picture had been of Michael mowing the lawn. One had been of her holding a starfish on the Oregon coast at sunset, another of Michael on horseback near Eagle's Nest at the start of their purchase.

The antique cradle had almost broken her.

"I can't have a baby, damn it," he said. "I'm not married."

"People do it all the time," she said flippantly and went to spin the dial.

He surprised her. Reaching out, he put his hand over hers. The spindle crushed into her palm, and she looked up to find very serious, very angry brown eyes. "*I* don't. If I'm going to have a kid, he's going to have two full-time parents."

Kat trembled. She'd never seen him so intense. "Do you want to quit, Michael? You're getting too serious. It's only a game."

"Is it?"

Kat was silent. She wasn't sure what to say.

"No," he finally said in answer to her question. "I'm not giving up now. I've got a child to support."

His mood improved after that. They played more, bantering as they did. Somewhere in that time Katherine began to lose badly, however. It seemed to her that after he got the kid Michael became unstoppable.

At last he starting nodding off. Katherine was determined to catch up and pass him, but he kept falling asleep. She kicked his foot to wake him.

"Take my turn for me. I'm too sleepy to read it," he said, yawning.

"'Cyclone wrecks home! Pay forty thousand dollars.'"

His eyes flew open. "I don't believe you. You put me there on purpose."

"If you don't trust me, you'll just have to stay awake," she announced.

He tried diligently for a few minutes, but he clearly couldn't succeed. At last he fell asleep again. This time when she kicked his foot she got no response.

"Hey, you. It's your turn." She kicked him again, this time a little harder. Still nothing.

"You're giving up," she announced, hoping he'd wake. She pushed her car to Millionaire Acres and added, "I win."

Nothing.

Michael's head was kinked in an awkward position, and she thought about adjusting it for him before deciding against the idea. He deserved to have a stiff neck in the morning; it would match his disposition. Kat smiled to herself, pulled her quilt around her neck and snuggled deeper into her beanbag. She supposed it was time to go to bed, herself.

She was almost asleep when something very disturbing dawned on her. She might be in Millionaire Acres, but Michael was the one with the baby.

Chapter Fourteen

Michael shivered in the darkness and pulled on the collar of the army coat he wore. It felt like his neck had been in a vise all night, and he had a roaring headache. He wondered when Kat had turned out the lights. The last thing he remembered was playing that silly game. He'd even dreamt of it. He'd pictured himself and Kat driving around in little blue plastic car with a passel of kids. Ridiculous.

Looking around, he groaned. That old buzzard of Kat's grandpa hadn't been kidding when he'd said he would see them in the morning. Michael just hoped Homer didn't forget about them. He supposed Celeste would remind him. He was surprised the woman had let Homer get away with locking them up here in the first place.

He staggered to his feet and pulled the string to the light bulb. Kat remained asleep. She looked comfortable, all curled up in her chair with that thick quilt covering her. She had a pleased look on her face, and Michael resented the hell out of that. He also resented how beautiful he still found her. He turned his head every which way, trying to ease the knots in his neck. Food, some coffee, a handful of pain relievers—that's what he needed. His watch showed eight-thirty.

"Come on, Homer. Get me the hell out of here."

Kat stirred and lazily opened her eyes. "Were you talking to me?"

"No," he said.

"Well, I see a good night's sleep didn't help your disposition."

"It wasn't a good night's sleep. Did you really think it would change my attitude, anyway?"

"No, I didn't."

His ex-wife stretched like a cat, all long and lanky and sensuous. Michael shut his eyes at the sight. Even with hair in disarray and her clothes crumpled and dirty, she looked exquisite. He supposed she always would, no matter what she did to him. He paced the room like a panther.

"Damn you, Grandpa. Hurry up." It was Kat who said that, and she was suddenly acting caged and agitated. The same way he felt.

"What's the matter? Has the princess had enough of the tower?"

"The princess needs to use the loo," she snapped. "I haven't had anything to drink for hours, but I need to go. Desperately!"

Michael groaned. "I wish you hadn't brought it up. Now *I* need to go. Let's try to keep our minds on something else."

"I've got a better idea," Kat said. "Let's make a plan for when Grandpa gets here."

"Why do we need a plan?" Michael asked. "The only plan I need is which bathroom to take."

"I get the upstairs. It's closer, and you can run faster than me. But we need to make Homer think we've worked out our differences or he's never going to let us out of here."

Michael tried to sound nonchalant. "We have worked things out. You're doing your thing, I'm doing mine. I'll finish the damn renovations and then be gone. It's for the best, which we both have known all along. You bought me for sex and carpentry. You got both."

Kat was staring at him. "Is that what you really want, Michael? Do you want me out of your life forever?"

Had she choked on that last word? Was this killing her as much as him? He took off the old coat he wore and threw it across the room. "I don't see any other way."

"Why?" she cried out, impassioned.

"Because you betrayed me, Kat."

"Betrayed you?" she repeated, clearly confused. "What about the times you let me down?"

He didn't want to go into it. Nothing had changed. They'd had their fun, now it was done. He'd have to see if her plan to conceive had succeeded, but after that they were through. It'd be best if he didn't talk to her; she only brought him pain. "It doesn't matter anymore."

Katherine jumped to her feet. "If it doesn't matter anymore, great! Let's drop the whole thing and start over."

He shook his head. "We can't, Kat. *I* can't. I guess what I meant to say is, it's too late. This just won't work for me."

# # #

Kat held her breath until she felt dizzy. What could she say to his argument? Michael didn't want her. It was simple as that, maybe it always had been. How could you argue with such a cold, hard, honest truth?

Of course, how could they be at this impasse again after all the love they had shared in the last few days? She wouldn't believe that any of their experiences and emotions had been anything but real. How could Michael change his mind in such a short time? She asked herself the question again and again, but she always came up with a blank. But if one of its actors wouldn't say his lines, your play couldn't have a satisfactory ending.

She collapsed back into the safety of her chair. It was nearer her center of gravity, and the position made her less nauseated. She wanted to cry, needed to throw up.

Swallowing back her sorrow, she tried to sound reasonable. "We still have to convince Homer that we have reconciled or he will never leave us alone. When he gets here, we must pretend like we are in love. Just until we get him out of here. Then you can leave."

"I'll finish the house renovations, too," Michael said. "We're almost done, and I won't go back on my promise."

"I can finish on my own," she growled. "Don't worry about it. With the situation the way it stands, with whatever you've decided to hold against me, I think it would be easier for both of us if you just left today."

He shrugged. "Suit yourself."

That casualness broke her heart. It was so much like the first time they split.

They heard footsteps coming up the stairs. Leaning close, Kat whispered, "Remember—if you can, pretend that you love me again until we get Homer gone. We don't want him doing anything else crazy like locking us in here. I've got to take him to the doctor this afternoon, and after that I'll send him home with Celeste and you can get out of here."

A moment later, Homer opened the door. "You two dressed?"

Kat flew to the entrance and pushed past him. Her plan had vanished in her sudden need to empty her bladder.

"What's going on here?" her grandfather called.

"Bathrooms," Michael explained as he followed her past the gaping old man.

A short time later, the four of them were seated in the kitchen around the table. Celeste was pouring coffee.

"I almost died on the way over when Homer told me what he did. He didn't mention a word about it last night. He said you two wanted some time alone, so we got our coats and left. You must be starved."

"I could eat almost anything," Michael agreed.

Kat's heart was so heavy she didn't feel like eating. She excused herself and went back to the bathroom. She threw more cold water on her face and brushed her hair. Wandering aimlessly to her bedroom, she lay down on her bed and hugged a pillow to her chest.

In one short day she had lost everything. No child. No Michael... She finally let her emotions take control, just for a minute, cried deep and laboriously into her pillow.

"Kat? Katherine?" She had no idea how long she had been there when she heard Michael and felt his hand on her shoulder, firm yet gentle. His weight depressed the bed, and the movement pulled the pillow away from her face. He saw her tears and said, "Babe, go wash your face or your Grandpa's going to know something's up. Breakfast is ready. I'll go tell them you'll be right there." He helped her to her shaky feet then left the room to make her excuses.

A short time later Kat entered the kitchen, trying her best to paste on a pleasant expression. "Smells delicious," she lied.

Everyone seemed intent on eating, and they didn't pay much attention to her. She was glad of it. Taking an egg, she demolished it with her fork, spreading it all over her plate so that it looked like she'd eaten something. A few sips of scalding coffee seemed to settle her nerves, and she broke off a piece of toast and munched on it.

"I'm not going to ask any questions," Homer said while taking another egg, "but I must admit, the air seems a little less hostile. You two act as if you've come to an agreement."

Michael turned to Kat and smiled, clearly waiting for her to speak. She didn't. The silence grew.

Michael gently kicked her under the table. When she looked up at him, his fake smile was getting strained. *Say something, damn it,* she saw in his eyes. *Lie.*

Kat was tired and hurt beyond words, and Homer was going to find out the truth very soon anyway. She knew she'd told Michael to play this charade, but she just didn't have the energy. If Michael wanted to fool Homer, he would have to do it on his own. It wasn't really likely he was going to lock them in the attic again. It wasn't even very likely they'd go up thcrc.

She took another gulp of coffee, and Michael's hand squeezed her knee under the tablecloth. It wasn't a gesture of endearment. When the silence lengthened, he cleared his throat.

"Everything's just as it should be, Homer. But, really, we could have worked things out just as well another way. You must admit that your action was a little drastic."

"Oh, don't go gettin' your shorts in a knot. My great-grandbabies will love hearing this story someday."

Great-grandbabies.

Kat stared down into her empty coffee cup, and she thought she heard Michael choke on his toast. She wanted to tell Homer right then and there that there weren't going to be any great-grandbabies, but she didn't have the strength to endure another of his lectures.

"Speaking of babies, I'd like to see what you've done with the nursery and the rest of upstairs. I didn't get much of a chance last night when I was up there."

"Too busy playing cupid?" Michael asked with a touch of sarcasm.

"Referee," was Homer's comeback.

"I want to see, too," Celeste stated. "I'll come with you," she said and removed her apron.

As the older couple walked up the stairs, Kat listened for them to reach the top before she spoke. Halfway up, however, Homer and Celeste stopped. Celeste's voice floated back.

"Are you all right, dear? Take it slow."

Michael and Kat exchanged a worried frown. Kat said, "I'm glad I made that appointment for this afternoon."

Michael dipped his head, his face taking on an odd expression. "It'll be a relief to know exactly what the trouble is."

Kat took a deep breath. She knew that tone of voice; she was about to get lectured.

"You're not acting this thing out worth a damn. Do you want Homer to chain us together or something?"

"Now there's a thought."

She was debating whether to give him a fuller answer when Celeste's frantic voice echoed down from the upstairs of the house. "Katherine, Michael, hurry! It's Homer!"

Kat took the stairs three at a time. Michael was right behind her. They found Homer lying on the floor of the nursery, his skin a sickly gray and his mouth the same shade as the ceiling.

"Oh, my God." She knelt down next to him. "Grandpa, where does it hurt?"

Homer didn't speak; he just clutched his chest. Celeste was staring at him, clearly unsure what to do.

"Stay with him, Michael," Kat commanded, running to the phone in the hallway and punching in numbers.

"9-1-1," a calm voice declared. "Is this an emergency?"

"Yes." What a stupid question.

"Hold one moment, please."

"You've got to be kidding. They put you on hold for 9-1-1?" But she was talking to dead air.

"Now," said the woman, returning and talking calmly as if taking an order from the Sears catalog. "What is your emergency?"

Kat explained the situation. The dispatcher finally got interested and promised to send an ambulance right over.

It was odd, the things you thought of in the middle of a crisis. Waiting for the dispatcher, Kat was reminded of the night of the auction, and how she'd felt while intending to purchase Michael for a week. She supposed that these moments were defining, and that was why they stuck in her head. These were the times that determined the rest of your life.

She replaced the phone back in its cradle and briefly wondered why it was covered in blue paint. That thought lasted only a brief moment, however, as she had to hurry back to her grandfather's side.

Chapter Fifteen

Homer lay very still in his hospital bed. Celeste sat on one side of him, Kat on the other. All the tests had been run, and now they played the agonizing waiting game. Kat knew her grandfather must be very ill; he hadn't said a word since his collapse. He was on a ventilator, however, and was breathing much easier.

"I'm so glad you're with us, Celeste," she said. "You've been such a good friend to Grandpa and to me. I feel like I've known you forever, not just for a few days."

The silver-haired woman gave her a smile. "I feel the same about you. I love your grandfather, Katherine." Her eyes clouded over, and she took Homer's limp hand in hers. "I know it sounds crazy because of the short time we've known each other, but I don't want to lose him just now that I've found him. He's a crazy old guy, but he makes me feel something that I haven't felt in years."

"What's that?" Kat asked.

"Alive."

Nothing else needed to be said. The two women completely understood each other. Their sad smiles across the bed were all-knowing.

Michael's head peeked around the door. "Are you two ready for a soda?"

"That sounds good, thanks." Kat wondered why he was still around, and yet somehow she also knew he wouldn't let her down in a time of crisis. But, why would she think that? Of course he would let her down. He was walking out of her life later today or tomorrow.

She didn't have time to think more about it, because the doctor came in. "Hello, Katherine." The doctor turned to Celeste and introduced herself. "I'm Barbara Noble."

Celeste stretched out her hand, and the two women shook. "I'm a friend of Homer's."

"Why don't we let Homer sleep," Dr. Noble said, "and we'll go to the waiting room to talk?"

The trio walked a short way to a cozy waiting room where the physician got right to the point. "Homer has congestive heart failure, like I feared yesterday. I know this sounds very serious, and it *is* if not handled properly. But if he'll take care of himself, he'll get along just great. With proper care he can live a few more years."

They talked of the symptoms and of the medication he would be required to take for the rest of his life. The doctor had a few questions about his early symptoms, and then she turned to Kat. "This came on quite rapidly. What time did we talk yesterday?"

Kat tried to remember. So much had happened since. "Let's see… I was fixing dinner when the phone rang, I'd say around five-thirty or six. But he seemed fine after that." She felt a sudden tinge of guilt. She didn't really know how Homer had been feeling. It was right after the call that Michael had started acting so strange.

The door to the waiting room opened. Michael entered, pushing it with his rear while juggling three glasses of soda with ice. His expression was serious, but when he was introduced to Dr. Noble his face took on a look of insolence. Kat noticed it immediately, as she was sure the others did.

Suddenly, it dawned on her—slowly at first, and then the last pieces fell into place and the full force of it hit her like a ton of bricks. In slow motion she saw everything in her mind: the phone ringing, Michael answering with wet paint on his hands. He must have listened to hear what the doctor had to say about Homer, and then he'd heard Barbara's innocent question at the end. *"Are you pregnant yet?"*

The newfound knowledge sent a wave of fear surging through her. If before this moment she'd had an ounce of hope, she had absolutely none now. No wonder he had turned on her so brutally. She had hurt him deeply. He had put his heart in her hand, and she had thrown it down and stepped on it. He would never trust her again.

She had to talk to him, had to explain how this whole mess had come about. Kat needed to tell him everything, from the conception of the idea with her friends to the exact moment she knew she couldn't go through with it. There was no hope in her mind that it would change anything, but he had to know the truth before he walked away forever. He couldn't leave without knowing her integrity had resurfaced in the nick of time. Time healed many wounds. Maybe someday they could at least be friends again.

Michael handed Celeste her drink, Kat hers without looking at her, and then, always the gentleman, he offered his own to the doctor.

"No, thank you," the woman said. "I've got patients to attend to. I'll check back in on Homer again before I leave for my office."

Celeste glanced over at Kat and Michael and excused herself. "I'll go sit with Homer. If he wakes up, I'll come and get you."

"Thank you," Kat said.

Michael sat down on the couch and sipped his drink. Kat put her straw in her mouth and sucked, but she found she didn't have enough room left around the knot in her throat to swallow. She set her glass down on the coffee table and reclined next to Michael.

"What's wrong with Homer?" Michael asked.

Kat explained what the doctor had told them as best she could. She had a hard time keeping her mind on the subject though, which added to the immense amount of guilt she was already feeling.

After she completed relaying the diagnosis, Michael seemed to relax. His dark eyes were cloudy with unshed tears. "That's great. God, I've been so worried about the old goat. I love him, you know."

Kat reached out an unsteady hand and touched his shoulder. "I know you do. And he loves you." She needed to say more, and this was as good a time as any. "Michael...?"

He looked directly into her eyes. She steeled herself and continued.

"Homer will always love you. Even though we're not going to be together, you and he should still have a relationship. You mean a great deal to him. I'm sorry I made him choose sides between us before. That was wrong of me. He needs you more than ever now— if you want to be there for him."

Michael bowed his head and stared at the carpet. "Of course I do. He was my only father and grandfather for years. I really missed him before the last couple of days."

There was silence then. Prolonged. It was time. Kat couldn't put it off any longer. She had to come clean with Michael before he left.

"Michael, there's something else I—"

Celeste burst through the door. "He's awake!"

Kat and Michael hurried after the woman into Homer's room. Kat's grandfather smiled when they burst through the door. The blue color in his lips had gone, and his cheeks were slowly regaining a pinkish tint.

"Grandpa." Kat laid her head on his chest. The steady beat of his heart was comforting. "You scared us to death!"

"It wasn't that fun for me either."

"How are you feeling now, dear?" Celeste asked. "You worried us all sick."

"Like I've been with a two-bit whore all night."

"Grandpa! Your mouth is going to get you thrown out of here," Kat chastised.

Michael laughed out loud. "He's better."

"Is that the Kid?"

Michael stepped close. "Well, Homer, you old coot, it looks like you're going to get to wear all of those hats after all. Here's another for the collection." He set atop the old man's head a new black cap with EAGLE'S NEST embroidered across the front. Then he took Homer's ancient hand in his strong young one and said, "I'm so relieved that you're going to be okay."

The room was silent. Everyone was thinking the same thing.

"It's not only the hats, Kid," Homer exclaimed after a moment. "I'm planning on being around to see my first great-grandbaby."

Michael glanced away before he turned back and engaged Homer again. In that moment, his eyes held a depth of sadness Kat had never seen before. Her own soul ached similarly, with a grief as strong as if she had just experienced the death of a loved one. To be honest, this pain might even be worse, because Michael would still be around, would fall in love with someone else and have that child Grandpa was talking about. And Kat knew beyond any other realization that she would never, ever, get over Michael. And now she had to tell him the truth.

Chapter Sixteen

Kat talked Michael into leaving the hospital and going to a quiet restaurant for dinner. She'd stayed with Homer first, while Celeste went home to freshen up and get a sandwich, but then Celeste insisted the two of them go out since neither had eaten since breakfast.

They chose the Weststar Inn, which a combination restaurant, bed and breakfast. The Weststar Inn was as charming as its name, furnished entirely with elegant antiques, and it had a menu to match. Michael and Kat had eaten there many times over the years, but this was their first time eating together there since the divorce.

The proprietor was surprised to see them together and tried to hide her astonishment. The woman took in their attire, which happened to be the working clothes they had put on the day before and slept in.

"Would the Blakes care for a private room this evening?"

"—No, thank you," Michael stated.

"—Yes, that would be better," Kat said.

They stumbled over each other's words.

Michael gave her an exasperated look; he clearly didn't want to be alone with her. Nothing would have changed because of Homer's illness or the fact that he wanted a great-grandbaby to bounce on his knee, so Katherine whispered an explanation as the owner led them upstairs to individual rooms.

"We're not dressed properly to mingle with the other guests."

Michael looked down at his paint-stained clothes and then at Kat's. "I guess you're right," he admitted with a shrug. Still, he looked antsy. She assumed he wanted to check on Homer once more and then get home to bed. If only this were a new beginning for them…but it wasn't.

They took seats in chairs on opposite sides of a beautiful Queen Anne table, and within seconds they'd ordered their favorite items from the sumptuous menu. The waiter appeared with a bottle of wine, and Kat took her time unfolding her linen napkin and smoothing it across her lap. Its stark whiteness looked silly against her dirty jeans.

She needed to approach this in just the right way; she didn't want Michael bolting from the room before she had time to explain everything. All the time she had been sitting with Homer she'd tried to think of the perfect way to begin, but she hadn't come up with a plan. Now, when she finally took a deep breath and spoke, her foray came out as clumsy as she'd been afraid it would.

"I know what you overheard on the phone yesterday."

Michael almost lost his grip on his wine glass, and he set it down gingerly. "Look, Kat, I don't want any explanations. I figured it all out for myself, and that was painful enough. I don't think I could stand to hear it straight from your mouth. Can we just drop the subject? Unless you're pregnant, of course. Then I guess we have a lot to talk about."

Kat shook her head. "No, no, I'm not pregnant. That's what I need to talk to you about."

"You don't want me to still *get* you that way, for God's sake!"

"No!" she said. "That's not it at all."

The waiter brought in green salads and disappeared again. Kat pushed the dish away. She had been hungry a minute earlier, but their conversation had her stomach topsy-turvy. It'd be a wonder if she ate anything at all.

"I need to tell you how this all got started," she said after a moment.

"I don't want to hear it," Michael repeated, shaking his head.

"I know you don't, but you haven't heard the whole story and you're going to let me tell you before we leave this room or I swear I'll follow you around like a dark cloud until you hear me out."

"Get it over with then."

Kat paused. "One disclaimer before I start."

Michael gave her a disgruntled look but didn't object.

"Before I continue, I know this won't change how you feel about what I've done. I guess what I'm trying to say is, I'm not trying to win you back. I just want you to understand the whole thing."

"I'm listening," he said. His face was stone.

"Okay." She took a deep breath. "As you know, I've wanted a baby for many years, and my time for having children is running short. If you remember, I always had pain during my period. It's endometriosis, it seems, and it's progressively gotten worse. Dr. Noble warned me the last couple of years that if I'm going to have a child, I'd better try sooner than later. She fears I don't have too much longer before I'll need surgery."

She took a deep breath. "I've tried to analyze what made me take such a drastic step as…as what I did to you. As what I tried to do. I'm not sure. I'd read several articles on single parenting, and on choosing the right father for your child, but there was no one in my life that I was remotely interested in having a child with." She paused, wondering if the truth would help or hurt her apology. "Except you. The night I saw your name advertised for the Make-A-Wish auction, I realized you were the one I wanted for the father of my child. The only one."

Michael just stared across the table at her. He said nothing.

"I brought the subject up to Georgi and Tara."

"Surely they weren't in favor of this silly scheme!"

"They had their reservations, but they support me no matter how crazy I am. They love me."

Michael shook his head. "You three have thought up some pretty hare-brained ideas, but this one—"

"I know. This one takes the cake. But when I saw your name in that ad, it was just too easy. I thought maybe it was an omen of some kind, that God or my Grandma or someone else in Heaven was telling me to go through with it. I know it sounds crazy. It *is* crazy, but I wanted it so badly that logic flew right out the window."

"But it didn't work, did it?" Michael said. Suddenly, he started to laugh.

Kat stared. Her heart was breaking, and he was laughing at her? The waiter brought their entrees and looked at Michael strangely as he did.

"I just thought of something," Michael explained between belly laughs. "What were you thinking when I pulled out that first condom?"

Oh. Kat's mouth twitched. She tried not to smile, but she couldn't help herself. "I wanted to kill you," she admitted.

"Then you would have *never* gotten pregnant." He laughed again. "And here I thought I was being such a considerate gentleman."

Katherine grinned in spite of herself.

"You know, Kat, if maybe we'd talked…"

She ducked her head and felt a blush rise to her cheeks. "I know. But to be totally honest, I didn't know what to say. And at that moment I was too emotionally involved with you to care about the baby." She didn't dare look at him. "I just wanted to be with you. Later I hoped there would be another time."

"And there was."

"Yes." She raised her head and smiled shyly at him. "Many."

He smiled back. A moment later he caught himself, and she watched him wipe the smile off his face.

"It was at Eagle's Nest with Jesse that I finally realized I couldn't do it to you—what I'd planned. I'd been having qualms the whole time, but when I saw you with Jesse I knew that I could never keep a child from you."

"Is that *really* what you planned to do? Get pregnant and then never tell me about my baby?" Michael's voice quavered with pain and rage.

Kat was silent. There wasn't much she could say.

"That's the part I can't figure out. The person I knew all those years ago would never even have considered such a thing. God, Kat! You know me better than that. I told you years ago that I never wanted to be an absentee dad like mine was. Didn't you know that I would want to be an everyday part of my child's life?"

"Yes, that was the problem, Michael. I assumed you would want to be part of its life—and that you wouldn't want to be part of mine, at least not in the way I need you to be. I didn't think of you, I barely thought at all. I wasn't myself. I let my selfish desire for a child cloud my judgment. But I realized what I was doing and gave up the plan. By the time we went to the cabin I knew that you were my number one concern, and I'd decided the baby should wait until we were both ready."

"The cabin." Michael looked questioningly at her. "You weren't trying to get pregnant then?"

"No. I put everything into perspective and decided not to worry about it."

"But, Kat, *that* was when we didn't use any protection."

"I know. But that wasn't even me! I wasn't thinking about that until later."

"Me, either," Michael admitted ruefully. "I was so caught up in that kiss—"

"It wasn't part of a plan," Kat promised. "It was all so romantic, what you'd done, and my only thoughts were of you and how happy I was to be with you again. I didn't think of the rest until later. I know that doesn't help my case, at least about my original intent, but I really didn't mean to—"

"Could you be pregnant now?"

She shook her head. "I don't think I am. It's too early to be sure, but what are the odds?"

"I always thought you'd be a wonderful one." His voice was very low. "Mother, I mean."

"Thank you."

# # #

Tears shimmered in Kat's eyes and Michael's heart went out to her, but he couldn't patch the hurt and tell her this was okay. It wasn't. He certainly held some responsibility for not using protection that night, but for her to plan what she had after all their difficulties, to lie and dissemble when they'd ended so terribly two years before… Yet, Kat's admission touched him deeply. He wished to God that he could simply forgive and forget. One part of him wanted to do that. The other just wanted to run.

"I appreciate you telling me, Kat. I know how hard this must have been, 'cause I've had a hell of a shock myself. You could have just kept quiet and let it all fade quietly into the past."

He looked down at his uneaten food and pushed it away. Excuse himself was what he should do, get out of there as fast as he could, go home to his condo and pick up his life where he'd left it the night of the auction. But he found himself comparing that stark condo to the toasty comfort of Kat's home. Maybe he should look into buying a house. But even as he thought about that, he knew the house wasn't what he craved.

"Are you through?" he asked, eyeing her untouched plate.

She sighed. "Yes." She didn't offer anything else.

"Kat." While he didn't want to say anything he would regret later, he had to tell her something of what he was going through. Their marriage had failed because they couldn't communicate; they both had to learn if they ever hoped to have successful relationships. He tried now to choose his words with care. "I'm sorry that things aren't working out for you, but I don't know you anymore. I don't know the part of you that could conjure up a scheme like this, whether you abandoned it or not. It makes me wonder who I've been dealing with—certainly not the woman I married."

She nodded, and one lone tear hit the cold pasta on her plate. "Of course not. And I'm sorry. I'd better get back to Grandpa."

Michael didn't press the point. He left a hundred dollar bill on the table to cover the bill, and they exited the Weststar quietly through a back entrance. They drove back to the hospital in complete silence.

When they arrived, Michael felt Kat take his hand and squeeze it. His heart stopped as she said, "Thank you, Michael, for all your help today. You can go home now. I know you must be exhausted."

"I'm sure you are, too. You don't plan on sleeping here tonight, do you?"

"Yes. I want to be with him."

He shook his head, not wanting her to punish herself, if that's what she was doing. "Kat, Homer's going to be fine. You saw him, and you heard Dr. Noble's prognosis. I think you'd better go home and get some sleep. You look like death warmed over."

"Thank you very much." She smiled sleepily at him. "Is that one of your famous come-on lines? I now see why the snow-bunnies flock to your resort."

Michael bit back annoyance. "I'm serious. Why don't you go in and tell him goodnight, and then I'll take you home. If you don't take care of yourself, you won't be able to take care of Homer," he reminded her. "You have to take care of yourself first."

She shook her head. "Thanks, Michael. I appreciate the concern, but I'm a big girl. I can take care of myself just fine."

That had once been something he believed. It had also been something he resented.

Chapter Seventeen

Early the next morning, Kat left Homer outrageously flirting with a nurse a third his age and drove home to get some much needed rest. Celeste was going to spend the day with Homer, and Kat promised she'd be back late that afternoon. She was bone-weary. Her body ached, and her emotions were so close to the surface that she was afraid she'd fall apart at any moment.

She switched radio stations three times on her way home. The first station wailed a country tune about a broken heart, the second a tender love song. When she flipped to her favorite classical station, the strains of Debussy's "Claire De Lune" almost sent her right over the edge. "Claire de Lune" had been her grandmother's favorite piece of music. A friend had played it at her funeral, and it had always been a gentle reminder to Katherine of the love her grandparents had shared. She knew she should change the station, shut the damn thing off, but she couldn't. She didn't have the strength.

Tears stung her throat, her head ached, and Kat wanted nothing more than to shut her eyes to the pain until it simply went away—until she vanished with it. But when the music came to her most beloved passage, the tender melody tore her in two. Kat could go no farther, although she was only a block from her home. She pulled to the curb on the narrow street, put the car in park, and cried until she could cry no more.

In a daze she drove to her house, parked in front and trudged wearily up the walk. She thought about fixing herself something to eat, but when she opened the fridge she changed her mind and wandered through the living room and into her bedroom. She wanted to simply flop into bed and never wake up, but as tired as she was Kat knew that she'd sleep much better if she had a bath first. It was only when she went to her dresser for a clean nightgown that she noticed the huge lump in her bed.

Startled, she ventured closer. Michael's golden head was partially covered with a pillow.

What was he doing here? When she'd told him to go home last night she'd meant to his own home. Why in God's green earth would he want to prolong this agony?

Kat had almost forgotten that her bath water was running, and she quickly ran to shut it off. She'd have her bath while the water was hot, and then she'd wake Michael and tell him to go home. Stripping off her filthy clothes, though, all she could think of was the man she adored lying for the very last time in her bed. Against her better judgment she wrapped a towel around herself and walked back into the bedroom. She had to have one last look.

He was sleeping soundly, deep even breaths making his chest rise and fall. Sorrowfully and with great tenderness, Kat brushed a lock of hair from his forehead and traced a gentle finger across his rough cheek.

"I love you, Michael. I'll always love you. And I'm so sorry for betraying your trust."

He didn't stir, but she felt a little better for saying what she had. She'd meant it.

She was just finishing her bath when she heard Michael up and moving around in the next room. The question of why he was there returned, as well as her sadness. She could hear he was preparing to leave.

Slipping on a pure white cotton nightgown, she wound a towel around her wet hair and walked into the bedroom. Michael was there wearing nothing but a pair of briefs, and he was straightening the sheets on the bed. He folded back one corner and turned to face her. His expression was unreadable.

"Right here," he said, patting the mattress. "Your turn."

Kat smiled. Even now, when she'd wronged him so badly, Michael had her welfare in mind. She dried her hair with the towel and brushed through it once; then, without a word, she did exactly what he had told her to do and crawled onto the bed. Reclining, she let out a long sigh and curled up in the fetal position.

Michael covered her and actually tucked her in. In another time and place he would have kissed her on the forehead, Kat knew, but in another time and place Michael might have crawled into bed and made love with her. But those times and places were gone now. She was so exhausted, however, she promised herself not to think about it for the next few hours. There was nothing to be done.

"Don't go to sleep yet," Michael cautioned. "You've got to eat something. I'm going to go fix you a big breakfast."

"No, Michael," she protested. "Really, I couldn't eat it. My stomach's a little out of sorts. A piece of toast and some tea would be just fine—just if you insist on anything."

"Okay. I'll be back in a minute."

She heard him moving about the kitchen and felt another wave of love for him. And yet, when she awoke he would be gone. He had to be. She didn't think she could deal with a long and torturous goodbye.

Outside, the teakettle began to whistle. Surprised at its speed, she listened intently a moment more. That was when she realized it wasn't the kettle. It was Michael. He was whistling!

He returned a few minutes later with tea and toast on a bed tray. "This should fix you up. And later I'm going to make you eat a full meal."

This was the time to tell him he didn't need to stay a moment longer, that he was free to go back to his other life. That he *should* go back to it. But somehow Kat couldn't or wouldn't let the words slip past her tongue. She simply ate her toast, sipped her tea, and smiled into the most incredible pair of brown eyes she had ever seen.

So, Michael had been whistling in there. He only whistled when he was happy and content. What had changed in him so dramatically from last night that he felt like whistling? Was it the fact that he was getting ready to go back home, or had he come to some separate realization? Was there a chance for them after all?

Kat fell fast asleep with that precious wish.

# # #

Afternoon sun filtered through the blinds, and Kat watched shafts of light dance across her bedspread. Once her sleepy brain began to wake, Kat listened for sounds of Michael in the house but all was quiet. Somehow, though, she couldn't conjure up the dread and despair she had felt earlier that morning. Maybe it was because she had finally acquired the rest she so desperately needed—or maybe it was because Michael had been whistling.

The clock on her nightstand said five-ten. She had slept the entire day. She needed to get back to the hospital, but her hair had to be rinsed again because she had gone to sleep with it wet and it was flying everywhere. She dressed and put on a little makeup, slipped into a pair of wool slacks and a cashmere sweater in mauve and gray. Just cleaning up made her feel one hundred percent better.

She wondered if Michael had finally gone home. Even if he had, she had the premonition that she would be hearing from him again. It had to have been the whistle.

In the kitchen she made herself a sandwich and poured a Diet Coke. She took both into the living room, switched on the TV and watched the national news. After that she brushed her teeth, grabbed her keys, purse, and coat, and opened the front door to leave.

Her car was still parked at the front curb. She wondered foggily why she hadn't pulled into the driveway, and then she remembered that Michael's Jeep had been there. In fact, it was still there. Where was he?

Kat's heart started pounding. He couldn't still be in the house, could he? She hadn't heard a sound. She turned around, put down her things, and went through the kitchen and up the stairs. This time her heart didn't just beat faster, it nearly stopped altogether, for as she entered the hall she could hear a soft whistle coming from the nursery. She moved to the doorway as if in a dream, and there she saw him on a ladder painting clouds.

Kat stood transfixed. She watched in fascination as one corner of the ceiling was transformed into a lovely summer sky. Billowy puffs of white dotted the blue background. They didn't yet have the depth and shading that were necessary, but that made no difference. Michael had stepped from his comfort zone, was trying something new and out of his realm of expertise. And he was doing it just to please her.

He turned, stepped down from the ladder and finally noticed her standing in the doorway. Pulling out earphones to his iPod he said, "Hi, you look much better. How do you feel?"

Kat just nodded. She was having a difficult time getting words to come out. She finally managed, "It's lovely, Michael."

"I figured I'd at least get it started. The longer you look at what a lousy job I've done, the sooner you'll get in here and finish it the way it should be."

Kat walked farther into the room, gazed up at the ceiling. She didn't think this was the appropriate time to ask him what he was still doing here; her timing with Michael had been off for days—years, for that matter. She was actually afraid to say much of anything, all for fear of making him pull away again.

Small talk. That would be best. Small talk.

"I've got the kite border down in the pantry. Should I run and get it so we can see how it looks?"

"Sure."

Michael moved up the ladder again, and Kat went in search of the border print they had bought three or four years earlier. As she rummaged through the closet, she rehearsed conversations in her mind. Every single thing she came up with to say seemed silly, however; teenager stuff. But when she thought of the serious questions she should ask Michael, her throat would constrict and she knew she'd never get them past her lips.

The bright colors of red, white and blue kites filled Kat's vision, and she reached for the package. A pang of remembrance threaded through her being as she did. She and Michael had been in Salt Lake for a day of shopping. She had thought she might be pregnant and told him while they were eating lunch. Michael had immediately insisted they go looking for baby things, just in case. They had purchased the border that day, though the pregnancy concern had been unfounded.

Kat mounted the stairs once again and stepped into the nursery. "I found it."

"Throw it up here." Michael caught the wallpaper, unwrapped it and held the sheet along one edge of the wall. "What do you think?"

"I think it's perfect. Just the finishing touch," Kat said. Her voice cracked, and she cleared her throat. "Michael, I really appreciate your finishing this project before you leave. Especially after everything I've done."

He set the wallpaper down and went back to applying white paint in fluffy cloud patterns. Without looking at her he said, "You know me, Kat. I hate leaving something undone. I've always liked to finish what I've started. I thought about it, and it seemed awful for me to not finish this project. I want to finish what you bought me for.

I owe you that much, no matter what happened. Especially since you 'fessed up and told me everything."

Oh. Was that all? He was almost finished here.

Kat wished she were a witch, so she could snap her fingers and put Michael's hands into slow motion, so slow that it would take him the rest of his life to complete those clouds. That didn't seem very likely, however.

"I need to get back to the hospital. Will you be here when I get back?"

"I doubt it," he replied. "I shouldn't sleep here tonight, and I really need to go over some things with Rona. We have some huge weekends coming up."

"Yeah," Kat agreed. "I need to concentrate on my shop, too. I've left Sandra in charge for almost a week now. She has plenty to do—she's been inventorying all of the new antiques I purchased over the last two months—but it's good if I'm there to help out. We have a busy time coming up with the Sundance Film Festival."

"Of course. We all do," Michael said. He climbed down from his perch and looked carefully at Kat. The air around them was full of paint fumes and tension. "I hear you're doing a great job with that store, Kat. I hear people talking about it all the time. You've made it a great success, and I'm proud of you. I wish I'd been there for the opening."

"Thank you, Michael. I appreciate that. And…and I wish I'd been there for the opening to Eagle's Nest." She really did. But what was past was past. Remembering all their various mistakes, Kat suddenly got sad. What were they doing to each other? Were they just going ahead and making the goodbye as long and painful as possible?

"Grandpa will be wondering what happened to me," she announced, steeling herself to leave. "Thanks again for all your help. Goodbye, Michael."

He didn't say anything, and she left the house in a rush.

"There," she said to herself as she reached her car. "That wasn't so hard, was it? You said goodbye and walked away." But it was with a violently trembling hand that Kat inserted the key and drove away from the house.

# # #

Kat could hear feminine giggles as she turned the corner of the hospital hallway leading to her grandfather's room. A chubby nurse in her mid-fifties was tucking the blankets in around Homer. Her nametag read Betty. Her round face was very pretty, and her smooth cheeks held a rosy glow.

"There now, Homer, you have a good night's rest. You should sleep like a baby after all the company you've had this afternoon."

"He's had a lot of company?" Kat asked.

Betty nodded and smiled. "Every nurse on staff has been in to see him at least once. He's such a ladies' man. I'll check in on you, dear, before my shift is over." She patted his hand then breezed from the room.

Kat wondered where Celeste had got off to, and how she'd taken Homer's flirtatiousness. "Another conquest, Grandpa? How are you feeling?"

"I feel fine—and stupid. I'm not sick enough to be in here. I'd leave tonight, but I'd hate to disappoint the girls. They expect to see me in the morning."

"Well, you can't let your fans down, Homer," Kat agreed, shaking her head. "I guess you'll just have to stay. Where's Celeste, anyway?"

"I talked her into going home. She looked tired, and I didn't want her worn out. After all, I'll be home tomorrow. I'll need a homecoming, if you know what I mean. She didn't argue too much, so I figure she's run off to bake me a cake."

"Grandpa," Kat said. "Maybe you ought to stop all this silly flirting—I mean, if you want to have a serious relationship with Celeste. Did you ever think that it might hurt her feelings? And I hope you're not insinuating that you might…that you would even consider…" Kat sat down in the chair beside his bed with an unladylike thud as she realized what he'd meant by *homecoming* a moment earlier. "Homer," she almost yelled, "don't you even think about sex!"

"That's like telling a frog not to think about flies."

"Dr. Noble said you were to take it easy," Kat reminded him.

From the twinkle in his eye, she knew his next statement before it escaped his mouth: "Easy is good. The man doesn't have to do all the work."

She huffed. "Somebody ought to tie you to a bed so you can't hurt yourself."

"Tied to a bed sounds fun, too."

"Grandpa! What kind of medication have they got you on?"

"Relax, young lady," her grandfather said. "I'm not on anything that's affecting my personality. But…I think you're right about hurting Celeste, so I'll back off of the flirting. I wouldn't want to hurt that beautiful lady for the world."

He didn't give Kat time to register her surprise, just switched topics and plowed ahead. "But let's talk about you for a minute. Do you know what your problem is? You're too uptight. Why don't you let your guard down a little and start enjoying yourself? If this little scare of mine has done anything, it's made me realize how short life is. I don't want to spend the rest of my days worrying about what I shouldn't do. I just want to have all sorts of fun and do exciting things so that I don't stagnate."

"Grandpa, being stagnant is one thing you're *never* going to have to worry about. If you haven't stagnated by now, you're never going to."

His face got dark. "Oh, hell, I know that. I guess I haven't learned a thing. It's not me I'm really worried about." He shifted to his side, facing Kat directly as he said, "It's you, honey. What's happening between you and Michael? I could see things weren't fixed when we got back the other morning."

Kat scraped her fingers through her dark locks. This was the last subject she wanted to get into, not right now and not with her grandfather. She didn't want to tell him the truth for fear of upsetting him, but she also knew she couldn't lie. Not to Homer. Not ever. No matter the whoppers or fibs or jokes he told others, he'd always gotten honesty from her.

When she was a small child, she'd stolen something from the local drug store and her grandfather caught her. Kat could still remember as if it were yesterday. It had been hot and muggy, and she and her best friend Susie walked downtown for a treat. Homer had given her a dime to spend, and the two girls each decided on a package of gum. They'd paid for their purchases and wandered over to look at the comic books when a friend of theirs from school came over to them, licking a Popsicle. The treat had looked so refreshing, and both girls looked at each other with discouragement. They had spent all their money.

Susie had said she was going to have one, anyway, and that they'd just bring back some money after dark and leave it under the mat on the front step. Kat readily agreed that it wouldn't actually be stealing, so when the lady at the counter went into the back for a prescription, the two girls each grabbed a Popsicle and scurried from the store.

Kat said goodbye to Susie at the corner, planning to meet her again later that day. She had just finished the first half of her treat and thrown the stick into the gutter when her grandfather met her on the sidewalk under a huge weeping willow.

"Hmm, that sure looks good, Katy. Is that what you bought with the dime I gave you?" Homer asked.

"Yep, and I got this too." Six-year-old Katy held up her pack of gum.

"All that for just ten cents?"

She'd looked up into the branches of the willow and sucked on the red ice. She didn't answer at first, and then she looked him square in the eye and said, "It was on sale."

She could still see the hurt on her grandpa's face, for he knew she was lying. "That's a great sale. I think I've got another dime, so why don't you walk back down there with me? I'd like to buy some gum and a Popsicle for ten cents, too."

Kat felt her tummy take the same little lurch it had that day so long ago. As they'd walked toward the store, her six-year-old heart had nearly stopped. And just before they entered the shop, Kat put a tiny hand on her grandfather's.

"I took the Popsicle, Grandpa. I didn't pay for it."

Homer hadn't said a word; he'd simply taken her hand and steered her home. When they were almost there he stopped her, squatted down to her level and said, "Katy, you will earn the money for that Popsicle by pulling weeds in the flower garden. When you have earned fifty cents, you will take ten cents to the store, give them the money and tell them what you did. I'll go with you. I want you to remember this one thing: You must always be honest, with other people and with yourself. If you can't do that, you will never be truly happy."

He'd never told her parents about the incident, and he'd never brought it up again. When she had pulled enough weeds, the two of them, his strong hand holding her trembling one, walked back to the store and did exactly as Grandpa had demanded. And Kat never forgot the lesson.

She didn't know how long she'd been sitting there with her thoughts when Homer asked her the question again: "Kat, what's happening with you and Michael?"

"Nothing." It was the most honest answer she could find.

"I know you love him."

Kat did nothing to deny the statement.

"And I know he loves you."

This brought Kat out of her silence. "That's not the case, Grandpa. I deceived Michael and hurt him badly. There might be a small part of him that still loves me, but he doesn't trust me anymore and there's nothing I can do to win back that trust. Because of my own stupid selfishness, I've lost him. Forever."

Homer scoffed. "Hogwash. What could you do that would be so rotten that he would walk away from the love of his life?"

Her time of reckoning was at hand. She hated to tell him, hated the repulsive words that must come from her mouth, but she did it anyway. "I tricked and seduced him and tried to get pregnant by him."

There. It was out. She waited for her grandfather's sharp intake of breath that never came. Finally, Kat looked up to see if he was still breathing. Homer lay in his bed, his tan and weathered face calm, regarding her with an even, gray gaze.

"And?"

"'And?'"

"Yeah. *And?* Why would he want to leave you for that?"

"Because I lied to him."

"I used to lie to your grandma every Thursday night when she asked if I had a beer at the bowling alley. She knew I was lying, she knew that I knew. I didn't try to cover the smell on my breath. Actually, I think she kind of liked knowing that her man had a tad bit of badass in him."

Kat rolled her eyes. "Grandpa, this isn't the same thing at all. This is serious. I wasn't going to tell him that he had a child by me."

"You're right. That is serious," Homer agreed, "but it's also the same. When you love someone like your grandma and I did, or like you and Michael do, you overlook some of the things that should bug the hell out of you about each other, or that might destroy an otherwise good relationship. You made a bad call, sweetie. I'll admit that. But Michael knows your heart as well as I do. He knows that you could never have gone through with it."

"I realized shortly after I started this whole mess that I loved him too much to go through with it. I decided that I just wanted to be with him. The rest could wait—forever if it had to."

"Did you tell him that?"

"Yes, but it was too late. The damage is irreparable."

"Bullshit," Homer grumped. "I wouldn't have locked you two up for the night if I didn't think you could work anything out. I should have done it two years ago, and I've been kicking myself ever since."

"It *is* too late, Grandpa," she insisted. "We've discussed all of this and it just isn't going to work."

"You are so close to having everything you've ever wanted in your life. So close." Homer's stare was intense. "I know Michael. I know men. There is a part of him that is fascinated by the tenacity you exhibited. You knew what you wanted, and nothing was going to stop you from going out and grabbing it. That's sexy, Katherine. It excites men—the right kind of men, anyway."

Homer pushed himself upright in bed before continuing. "You chose Michael to be the father of your child when you could have picked anyone in the universe. You don't think that's an ego boost? I still remember the first time you brought him to our house. He couldn't take his eyes off you, and I could see that he adored you just like I did your grandma. I also never saw you act so alive and confident as you did with Michael. With chemistry like the two of you have, magic happens. And yes I said 'have,' because it's still there, Katherine. Get out of your own way so that you can see what's in front of your face."

Kat thought about her grandpa's advice. She thought about Michael whistling and sticking around her house to finish the renovations when he'd had every right to flee. "Maybe you're right?" she allowed querulously.

"Of course I am."

She bit her bottom lip as she weighed her options. "All right. I've been passive long enough. It's time I tell Michael that I need another chance. I've apologized, and he knows my heart. If he turns away, at least I've done everything I could to patch things up. It won't be like before, two people moving quietly away from each other. This time it's sink or swim."

"Atta girl," Homer said. "It's always better to go down swingin'."

Chapter Eighteen

"I hope you don't mind coming back into work so late, Rona," Michael said as he poured himself and his assistant cups of coffee. "We have a couple of things we should tackle, especially about that possible Swiss deal, but I must confess I really didn't need your help as much as your advice, and this isn't something I want to discuss over the phone."

"No problem," Rona said. "My daughter is spending the night at a friend's, and I just planned on chowin' down on pizza while lusting over Sean Connery."

"Isn't he a little old for you?"

"That's the beauty of movies. He can be any age I want him to be."

"I'm sorry if I ruined your date with Sean."

"You haven't. You ruined my date with *Robert.* When I get through here I'll just plug Sean back into the DVR. That's what I love about these platonic relationships of mine. I can have my men at the touch of my fingertips, anytime I want, for just 99 cents."

Michael snorted, amused. "What movie did you rent?"

"*Medicine Man*. Love that ponytail."

Michael looked at her. "A ponytail? Why do women get so turned on by that?"

"I think because we all want to be taken by a 'primitive man.'"

Michael shook his head. "I don't understand you females at all. You expect males to be gentlemen—kind, caring, loving—and yet you want an animal in bed."

"Now, I didn't say 'animal,' exactly. I said 'primitive.' There's a difference—but don't ask me to explain it. That's just a little too private to be discussing with some kid I used to babysit." Rona changed the conversation abruptly. "Michael, what's wrong?"

He glanced up at her, and her face was full of concern.

"I really appreciate you always being there for me, Rona. Do you know that?"

"Sure I do. I feel the same way about you. Now, talk."

"I don't know where to begin." Michael tapped the end of a pencil on the smooth surface of his desk. "This all seems so silly and sordid when I say it out loud."

"The expression on your face doesn't say you think it's silly," Rona said. "Tell me what's going on. You're beginning to scare me."

Michael breathed deeply and began. "Kat didn't buy me at the auction just so that I could finish the house."

Rona laughed. "No kidding. Don't tell me you're surprised at that?"

"No," he admitted slowly. "I guess I'm not surprised about it, but I am shocked by her real intentions."

"Which were?"

"To seduce me so that she could have a baby."

The lift of Rona's eyebrow was the only sign that she might be amazed by the revelation. "My, my. The little girl grows up."

"Grows up!" Michael repeated. "How do you come to that conclusion? I think this is the most juvenile, outrageous scheme she's ever concocted!" He broke his pencil into two pieces.

"It's outrageous all right, but it's hardly juvenile."

"Look. I know that Kat's wanted a family for years. She thought I was going to be a part of that dream, and when things fell apart for the two of us she decided to go about getting the part of her dream that she could still make come true."

Rona nodded. "Sounds like she grew up—or at least she decided to fight for something. She set out to get what she wanted."

"But at whose expense? Mine. It was utterly selfish of her, Rona. She didn't think of my feelings for a moment. She wasn't even going to tell me about the baby! That isn't right. I'd want to be as much a part of our child's life as she would. I have every bit as much to offer as she does, and every bit as much right to be a parent." His voice caught in his throat and he couldn't go on.

"You're right, Michael." Rona talked softer, though she stayed in her chair across the room. "You would make a great father, and you have every right to know if you ever father a child. But I think you're forgetting something."

Michael looked up.

"Kat loves you. She's always loved you. Your friends have always known it. We watched you both screw up—no, don't deny that you should have given her a *bit* more time while building this place—and we watched you both react to each other's mistakes. Badly. It all just snowballed out of control, and after the separation you were so closed to discussing it, and Kat made us promise not to talk about it… It's been awful to watch you two hurt so badly, knowing there was nothing we could do about it."

Michael didn't deny any of it. He knew that things could have been handled better during their first attempt at marriage, and he was willing to take some of the blame, but that didn't change the fact Kat deceived him in a way that went against his core. She knew what being a true, honorable father meant to him.

"Then why, Rona? How could she do it?"

His friend shrugged. "I don't know for sure. I haven't talked to her about it. But sometimes when a person can't get his or her life together in just the way they plan, and they have a strong emotional bond to the goal, they take an alternate route that seems a little out of character."

"It was definitely out of character for her. I don't even know the part of her that would consider doing that." Michael grimaced and tried to relax by putting his feet up on his desk.

"Did she go through with it? Is she pregnant?"

"No. She says she's not. At least, she doesn't think so. She told me she reconsidered her actions and couldn't go through with it, but…" Michael hesitated, thinking of their day and night together at the cabin. "She could be pregnant, I guess. We weren't all that careful." He pushed a hand through his unruly hair.

"Well, she'd know," Rona reassured him. "Anyway, Michael, Kat had a lapse of judgment. We all have times when we're desperate and make mistakes. She pulled it together before anything happened, right? And while she *said* she'd planned not to tell you if she was pregnant, she didn't actually do that. She didn't vanish into thin air, and it even seems like she was making an attempt to have a relationship again. So I guess what you need to ask yourself is if you're too hurt to try that out."

Michael threaded his fingers together and pressed them to his lips.

Rona continued. "Let me put it another way. Are you willing to live the rest of your life without her, all because of a desperate idea she had and didn't follow through on?"

"The rest of my life?" he repeated. Somewhere, somehow, Kat had always been a part of his dreams and goals. After the divorce he'd realized he would have to rearrange those dreams, but really he had focused on creating Eagle's Nest, a dream they had once shared. He'd even spent an incredible amount of time making sure her ideas were implemented.

"No, I'm not willing to live without her in my world. Not because of that." And then, very softly he added, "I can't imagine a life without her."

Rona, wise friend that she was, remained silent.

"All my life I've had a hard time trusting people. I figure it's because of my dad leaving us when I was a baby, and then my mother promised to always be there for me and died. From thirteen until the day I met Katherine I didn't believe in much of anything or anyone, but she changed all that." Michael felt a wall within him, and hope surging behind it. "I've just got to trust her and the love we've shared to pull us through. I have to *always* do that. I love you, Rona."

His friend laughed. "That's a good start, but her name is Kat." She smiled. "Go now. Don't wait until morning. Go tell her how you feel."

Michael put his feet on the floor, stood up and grabbed his coat. As he moved toward the door, he stopped and kissed Rona on the top of her head.

"Don't," she commanded, "get into a car wreck on the way over there or something equally corny. Take your time, the roads are icy. I don't want you ending up like Deborah Kerr and Cary Grant. It took them *forever* to get together. It drove me nuts!"

"I have no idea what you're talking about," Michael said.

"Of course you don't, dear. You're a man. But I won't hold it against you. Now go."

Michael left Rona to lock up the office. He wondered if Kat would be at the hospital or at home. More importantly, he wondered what the rest of the night would bring. And the rest of their lives.

# # #

Kat drove home from the hospital in a rush. She had to see if Michael might possibly still be there, had to talk to him before she lost her nerve. Homer's logic had made sense to her, at least while he was talking, but could she confront Michael and ask for one more chance? Would he even pay attention?

Disappointment filled Kat as she approached the house. Michael's Jeep was gone. She was too late.

No. She'd never give up. Without a moment's hesitation, she put her car in gear and careened down the icy streets and out of town toward Eagle's Nest.

Michael drove past Kat's house, but when he didn't see her car there he kept on driving down the road toward the hospital. He parked the Jeep and walked briskly through the halls to Homer's room.

The door was shut, and Michael wondered if Katherine might be resting inside, sacked out in the chair alongside Homer's bed, but when he knocked, the voice that welcomed him wasn't Kat's or Homer's.

"Come in?"

Michael did so. A cute blond nurse in her early twenties smiled up at him and then looked back to Homer.

"Hey, Kid, what are you doing here?"

"I came to see how you are, ol' man, but I see you're doing just fine." Michael grinned, considering the nurse standing protectively by Homer's bed. "And," he continued, "I'm looking for your granddaughter."

"She left here about twenty minutes ago."

"Did she say where she was going?"

"I thought she was headed home to talk to you. Mitzi, honey?" Homer addressed the young girl. "Would you run and get me a cup of ice and a Coke?"

"Of course, Homer. I'll be right back, and then you must finish that story about your days as a real live cowboy."

"Sure, sweetie."

Michael's jaw twitched with amusement as the nurse excused herself. "A real live cowboy?"

Homer didn't have the prudence to look guilty. "She's a cowgirl from Heber. She listens to country music and wears Wranglers when she's not in uniform. She was an all-state barrel racer, and her horse's name is Gilbert."

"You sure know a lot about her, Homer."

"Well, you just have to ask the right questions. I decided to tell her what a *true* cowboy was like."

"But you weren't ever one, were you?"

"No, but I knew a couple."

Michael shook his head.

"What difference is that little lie gonna make?"

"So that's where Kat gets her audacity," Michael said under his breath.

Homer ignored him. "I get to enjoy telling a good story, and the girl gets to take a memory home with her to share with her family and friends. What's wrong with that?"

"I don't know, Homer. Maybe there's nothing wrong with that, and maybe there's a lot wrong with it. Making people think you're something you're not can be very harmful."

Wow, Michael realized. Here they were, right at the core of the conflict.

Homer got an odd look on his face. "I guess you're right, Michael," he confessed. "Katherine tried to be someone she wasn't for a while, and you learned about that. But what's important here is that she discovered all on her own that she really couldn't be anything but the caring, sensitive, person she's always been. Just like Mitzi is about to learn that she should stick with her boyfriend of three years when part of her thinks he's too good to her. I just thought she'd want to hear it from a real life cowboy. Give her a sense of home, you know. Not everyone has the sense to listen to the wisdom of their elders."

Michael was more than a little surprised—both that Homer was dispensing relationship advice and that Kat had confided in her grandfather about the baby situation. "I guess we all push the edge, Homer. I do, Kat did… I guess if you never lose sight of the shore you can't get to the other side."

"Damn straight. Now get out of here so I can fix Mitzi's relationship. I have to do that before Celeste comes back. Don't want her being jealous or nothin'."

Michael walked to the door and then turned back to face Homer. "Kat took a risk—a big risk. I guess now we'll have to decide if it was worth it or not."

# # #

Kat didn't see the truck pull out in front of her until it was too late. On the treacherous road she knew she should have pumped her breaks instead of slamming on them, but her foot reacted from instinct rather than logic.

It worked. She didn't hit the truck, but her car spun out of control on the lonely road leading to the resort. The driver of the truck that caused the problem didn't even seem to notice that she'd almost hit him, let alone that she was in trouble. After three complete rotations down the middle of the deserted street, Kat held her breath as her car finally came to a halt in a snowy ditch. The sudden stop jarred her back and neck a little, but other than that she wasn't hurt.

"Great. This is perfect. Ten o'clock at night, all alone on a snowy country road, car in ditch, five miles back to town and two miles straight up to Eagle's Nest."

She looked down at her clothes. They might be adequate for the cold, but her high-heeled boots would never do in these conditions. But she did have to walk for help. She wasn't about to sit here all

194

night. She could freeze to death, maybe. Foolishly she had taken a closer back road into the resort, and it could possibly be hours before someone drove this way.

Actually, she had enough gas to keep her warm for several hours. But she'd had a much different night in mind, and she desperately wanted to get to Michael and talk him into giving her another chance. She hadn't even bothered to grab her phone or a pair of gloves when she'd left the house; she'd had too much on her mind. In fact, that's why she'd slid off the road. She wouldn't ever admit it to anyone, but she'd been putting on lipstick in her rearview mirror when the truck pulled out. She had no one to blame but herself.

Again. Was this some kind of a self-defeating pattern?

After buttoning her coat and throwing her purse over her shoulder, Kat stepped out the car. Her boots immediately sank into deep wet slush. She rummaged through her purse for the penlight Homer had given her last year; she'd never used it before and wondered if it were still there. Her fingers touched metal, and she pulled the tiny gold cylinder out and pushed the button.

"It works," she said out loud to the silent evening. "But I'd have to be an ant to get the full benefit."

Her boots had absolutely no traction as she moved from the ditch to the road, and Kat took one step onto the glassy surface and fell flat on her rear. Pain flooded her left buttock and she lay there in the middle of the road until the freezing ice stung her hip. She pulled herself gingerly to her feet. Now her wool slacks were wet and far from warm, her wrist was aching—she must have tried to break her fall with it—and her left hip burned like crazy.

She looked up and down the narrow, winding road. After a minute's deliberation, she opted to walk toward Eagle's Nest. Going up would mean a steep hike, but on these slick roads going down could mean slipping and sliding clear to town, something Kat was too sore to consider. She was several feet from her car when she realized the front end of her bumper was partially blocking the road; if someone rounded the corner fast, they would very likely run into it. So she trudged back and turned on her emergency flashers. That would help until the battery ran out.

Kat waded up the deserted highway looking for landmarks that might tell her exactly where she was. The signs were covered with a thin layer of sleet, and there wasn't enough light to see them. None of the signs had lights. Michael didn't want anything neon cluttering up his mountain. Everything had been designed with extreme good taste.

She wondered where Michael was. He had left her house, so she figured he had gone back to his own home. It was getting late. He had probably taken a shower and gone to bed.

Kat's fingers were tingling with the cold. She tried walking with her hands in the pockets of her coat, but she kept losing her balance so she alternated each hand every few minutes, tucking one under her armpit until it warmed up and then switching to the other.

It had started to snow. Just her luck, the flakes came down in pelting chips of ice. Her slick boots made it nearly impossible to keep trudging up the icy hill, too. She was cold, tired, wet, hurting, and to top it all off, she had to get to a bathroom again.

Kat detected a hint of light in the black sky, and as she rounded the next corner she was sure that she was getting closer to the resort. The sky ahead had paled a shade or two, and in only a hundred more yards Kat felt faint beams of light welcome her. She knew she had a long way to go, but the greeting warmed her insides.

Kat heard the vehicle before she saw it. She moved off to one side, getting out of the way while making herself conspicuous enough to be seen. Maybe the driver would stop and give her a ride. In fact, Kat waved an arm as the headlights blinded her.

The four-wheel drive stopped only inches from her feet. "Kat?"

Michael's voice had never sounded sweeter to her in her entire life.

He was by her side instantly, putting a warm, dry arm around her damp shoulders. "Are you all right?"

"I'm fine. Some jerk pulled out in front of me and I lost control. Well, it was my own fault and I—"

"I saw your car there, and when I couldn't find you I thought you must have gotten a ride. I had no idea you'd be out in this. Why didn't you call me?"

"I left my phone home," she muttered.

"And your gloves I see. You know better than that, Kat. Who goes out in January in Utah without those things?"

"Someone who has a lot on her mind!" Kat snapped back.

Michael tucked her into the passenger side of his Jeep and shut the door, and in just a few short moments they were pulling into his parking stall off to the side of his condo. He opened her door and escorted her up the walk to the front door. Kat couldn't help but enjoy the attention.

"How did you get behind me?" she asked. "I went by the house and you were gone."

"I went to see if you were at the hospital."

"You did?" Kat wondered what he'd wanted to see her about, but she didn't ask. She didn't want to be derailed from her intention of throwing herself on his mercy.

"Homer seems to be doing great. We had an interesting visit."

Kat was suddenly worried. "Oh, really? What about?"

"Just man talk. But it's good to see that he's back to normal—or even better than. He seems really into Celeste. I mean, *really*. I never thought I'd see that day." He shook his head and laughed. "Oh, but we need to figure out about your car. I'll call one of the guys, have them pull it out with the tractor and bring it here. Was there any damage?"

"No, it's just stuck," Kat admitted.

"Good. There's a robe hanging on the back of the door in the bathroom. Go get out of those wet clothes, and then we'll determine the extent of your injuries."

It wasn't the way he said it as much as the words he used, but she laughed. "Yes, Dr. Blake. May I shower, or do you want to examine me first?"

Michael had moved to the kitchen and was putting water into a kettle. "I ought to spank you, you little brat."

Her heart missed a beat. Before she could think about what his words might mean, she blurted, "Sounds fun." Then she fled to the bathroom and shut the door.

Inside, safe and warm, Kat stripped off her soggy clothes and stepped into a hot shower. He hadn't suggested she take one, but she knew she needed another few minutes to gather her wits. Michael's condo was elegant and clean, and luxurious places like this had always been a big turn on for her. She finished scrubbing, towel-dried her hair, wrapped Michael's robe around her and went to find him.

"I'm ready, doctor," were somehow the first words out of her mouth. She sat down on a barstool across the counter from him where he stood in the kitchen.

Michael grinned. He handed her a mug of coffee and asked, "Did you say you wanted to play doctor?"

She shook her head, hoping her eyes would tell him everything she was feeling. Did she need to prostrate herself if they were already on the same page? His eyes were so warm and kind, he'd been so solicitous since picking her up… And what had he wanted to talk to her about?

"No," she said slowly, "I want *you* to play doctor. I'll be your patient."

Michael set down his cup and moved around to Kat. He took her seat in both of his hands and spun her to face him. Boldly pushing her legs apart, Michael eased his body in close to hers.

"Where does it hurt?" he asked in a husky whisper. "Here?" He kissed the taut cord on the back of her neck, and instinctively Kat arched her breasts toward him. A rough hand cupped one and he rubbed a nipple with his thumb. "Or here?"

"Here," she told him, and pointed to her heart. "And here." She indicated her pouting lower lip. His lips ravished hers, and Kat's toes curled around the rung of the stool.

"There, is that better?"

Still reeling from his seductive kiss, she could only nod.

"Do you have any more owies?"

He seemed intent on taking care of her, and suddenly Kat remembered the injuries she'd sustained in her fall. She lifted her limp wrist, and Michael held and kissed it tenderly. Next she untied the robe and pushed the thick fabric away from her side. She wanted to show him where she'd sat down hard.

Michael's eyes traveled down to her buttocks and he exclaimed, "God, Kat, you really are hurt. Look at that bruise."

Kat saw that her skin had indeed changed color, turning an ugly shade of blue.

"What happened?"

"I fell on the ice when I started walking."

"Why didn't you tell me that you fell?" He didn't wait for an answer, just touched the wounded area and looked concerned. Then, in a gentle yet erotic move, Michael knelt down and kissed the bruise.

"Any more?" he asked, staring up at her from his knees.

Kat nodded her head like a little girl saying yes to a lollypop. She started pointing to every part of her body that needed one of those delicate kisses.

The doctor obliged.

In one way their lovemaking was sweet. In another, there was an urgency, an almost desperate attempt to capture something they had lost or were losing. Afterward Kat was disappointed in herself that she hadn't spoken to Michael before falling back into bed with him, but everything seemed to be happening backward. She knew making love had not resolved their problems, and just because she was lying in his arms right now didn't mean that they were back together.

"Michael? Michael, wake up. We need to talk."

Michael groaned and turned his back toward her. "Tired," he grunted.

"Hey, come on," she insisted, tugging on his shoulder.

"It's the middle of the night," he reminded her in a husky tone. "I don't do conversation well at three a.m." He rolled onto his back and slid a strong arm under her neck, gently pulling her toward him. His warm mouth covered hers, and for a few minutes of sweet rapture Kat forgot everything else. But when his strong hand slid up to cup a breast, Kat's resolve returned.

"Not so fast, my love. We've got some things to work through, and we can't solve every problem with lovemaking." She gently removed his hand, reached over to the bedside lamp and turned it on. Michael's eyes squinted shut, and he pulled a pillow over his head, but she continued undaunted. "When the lovemaking is over, the problems are still there."

Michael pushed the pillow from his face and turned to face her. "Okay, Kat. Talk."

Now that she had his attention, Kat didn't quite know where to start. "Before I get into all this, first I must tell you that above everything else I love you. Everything I've done lately, everything I haven't done…well, it's all been because I love you and want to be with you."

Michael's face got serious. "Really, Kat? It's all about that?" He sounded like a little boy, hopeful, terrified, and it touched Kat to the center of her very soul.

"I've never been so sure of anything in my life. I love you, Michael, more than I've ever loved anyone or anything. I'm so sorry for trying to trick you, and you must believe that I would never have gone through with having your child and not telling you. I know that deciding to have a child should be a joint decision, and I promise that we'll make that decision together when the time is right."

Michael cut in, "If we get back together, I think that we'll need some time to work on our own relationship before we think of having a baby. We've got some wounds to let heal. I love you, but there are things we're going to need to fix. And I've always believed a child should be conceived in wedlock. I know it sounds old-fashioned, but that's how I feel."

Kat heard what Michael was saying, but her heart stopped as he said he loved her. Even during their intense lovemaking Michael hadn't said those words, and now he slipped them into conversation as if they were commonplace. But hearing it from him after all this time was music to her ears.

She almost hated to ask the question, but she wanted to hear the words again. "Did you say you loved me?"

Michael brushed a lock of hair from her cheek and looked deep into her eyes. "I love you, Kat, very much. Always have. And I do want to have a child with you someday. I honestly could have strangled you a few times over the past few days. I was hurt and disappointed by this scheme, and yet I was honored and proud that you chose me to be the father to your baby. And I'm even happier to learn that it's because you never stopped loving me. It's a complicated thing we're in here."

"It doesn't have to be, Michael," Kat promised. "We can take our time readjusting to each other and work on the rest later. For right now, let's just concentrate on the two of us."

"It may not be easy," Michael pointed out. "Even if we agree to work on it now, tonight, we have to be ready for tough times. I've gotten used to a different lifestyle, and I'm sure you have too. I travel quite a bit now, and you've got your shop. Do you think it's possible to combine lifestyles?"

"People do it every day. If we love each other and we're committed to making this last, I think we can do it. We can do anything."

Michael searched her eyes. His words were gentle, but they still stung. "We thought that the first time. What's going to make this different?"

Kat had asked herself the same question. She thought she had an answer. "For me the difference is that I've matured. My priorities have changed. I know what's important to me, and I'm willing to do whatever it takes to get the things I want."

"Like seducing your ex to have his baby?" Michael's mouth held a half-smile, and he tweaked the tip of her nose. "I still can't believe you would try such a thing. You've always been somewhat unpredictable, but this was far beyond anything you've ever tried. What got into you?"

"It's a woman thing," Kat said, shaking her head. "There was a part of me that rationalized the whole plan because I was 'doing it for the sake of my unborn child.' But when I saw you walk out onto that runway, I knew without a shadow of a doubt that no other woman was going to take you home."

"Is that so?" Michael asked, taking her swiftly in his arms. "And what if someone bid five thousand dollars?"

"She could have bid ten thousand and I would have found a way to keep you. I'm not sure how, but I would have. Trust me."

Her last two words hung in the air. It all boiled down to this. Kat knew she had to be trustworthy for Michael, but in order to do that successfully, first she had to trust Michael in return—trust him to be there for her no matter how difficult things got, trust him to be always looking out for their best interests, trust him to talk to her when things got rough. And she needed to talk to him.

In the security of Michael's embrace she was positive she could do it. "I trust *you*, Michael. Completely."

Chapter Nineteen

They made love again that night. The next morning, Katherine rose quietly from Michael's bed and dressed. She kissed him gently on the cheek and left him a note saying that she had to pick up Homer from the hospital but she'd call him after lunch. She couldn't wait to see him again.

Michael had been as good as his word; as she stepped into the fresh, crisp air, Kat saw her car was parked next to his. The storm had passed, and she smiled at the blue sky above. After a quick inspection she decided her car was all right to drive, backed carefully out of the driveway and worked her way down through maze of the condos, onto the road that had caused her so much grief the night before. Turning toward town, Kat felt the sun kiss her cheek and she smiled once more. Life could be so very good sometimes.

She looked at the clock on her dashboard. Homer was being released from the hospital at ten, and it was already after nine. She'd called Celeste and told her it'd be better if Homer stayed with her for a few days; she just couldn't bring herself to trust Homer to take care of himself. The man could resist anything but temptation.

She decided to go to her house first and change. She would just have enough time. But just as she opened the front door, her cell began to ring. She rushed to her bedroom and sat down on the edge of her mattress.

"Hello?" she answered breathlessly.

"You sound like someone kept you up all night."

Michael's deep voice was husky and soft, and the sound of it made Kat's pulse quicken. "You sound like you're just waking up. Are you?"

"I am. I'll confess, I had a vixen in my bed last night, and she's worn me to a mere shell of the man I was yesterday."

"And she'd like another performance very soon, if possible."

"That can be arranged," Michael said. "How about tonight?"

"Oh," Kat said. "Homer will be staying with me for a while. It's best for his health, but I'm afraid it might put a hitch in our…time together."

"Do you mean our *intimate* time together?" There was a chuckle in Michael's voice.

"Yes, that's exactly what I meant."

"Where is he going to sleep?" Michael asked.

"In my room. There isn't anyplace else I feel comfortable putting him. He needs a bed."

"I'll finish up my work here and be over later this afternoon. Pretty quick I can have that extra bedroom fully finished, we can get the tools out of there and put a bed in for him. I'm sure I have an extra one hanging around the resort that could do if necessary."

"That would be great. Thanks, Michael."

"Don't thank me. Thank my desire to sleep with you." She could almost hear his smile. "By the way, Jesse called this morning."

"I wish I would have been there," Kat said. She was reminded of how cute Michael had been with the boy. "How is he?"

"He's doing great. He just chatted a bit and then confirmed our email addresses. He said he would write soon."

"He's an amazing kid, and I am happy to call him my friend." Kat cradled the phone in her hands, not wanting to hang up. It didn't seem to matter how much time she spent with Michael, she always wanted more.

Michael seemed to feel the same. "I love you, Kat. I miss you already."

"I love you, too." Katherine shut her eyes and enjoyed the moment. Times like these made life worth the struggle. Then: "I guess I'd better get to the hospital. I was supposed to pick Homer up at ten, so he'll be chomping at the bit. Especially after he finds out he's not going with Celeste. Can I call you after I get him settled in?"

"Don't worry about it. I'll be over as soon as I'm through here. I'll see you then."

Kat hurriedly changed her clothes and left for the hospital. When she arrived, Homer was indeed agitated, as she'd expected. He was sitting in a wheelchair in the waiting room with a smiling nurse standing behind him.

"It's about time. They were just getting ready to move me to the morgue."

"Relax, Grandpa, I'm only ten minutes late. I'll have you home in no time."

Kat ignored his snort of disgust and went to the main desk to sign the necessary papers. Within minutes they were out the door and into the car.

"Where am I going to sleep if I stay at your house?" Homer questioned.

"In my room, and I don't want any arguments about it," she said sternly. "I don't want you going to Celeste's until I know you're okay."

"Celeste can take care of me as well as you can."

"I know that," Kat admitted, "but you're my grandfather. I should be the one taking care of you."

"Is that it?" he argued. "Are you afraid somebody might not think you're a good granddaughter if I don't stay with you? Or are you afraid of a man actually having a good time in his old age? Why

I could tell you stories about me and your grandma that would put a high blush on your cheeks!"

"Okay, that's enough. Good grief, you're obnoxious today. I think you need a nap."

"There you go again, talking to me like I'm a child. You're going to make a wonderful mother," he snapped. Then he saw the hurt in her eyes and his voice softened. "Kat, honestly, you *are* going to be great. I just wish I was going to Celeste's."

Kat made no comment. She wondered if that were really true: Would she make a good mother someday?

"Did Michael find you last night?" her grandfather asked.

"Yes," she said, and thinking of their hours of lovemaking she smiled. "Yes, he found me."

"How did it go?"

She really didn't want to talk about it. Not now at least. Not with her grandfather.

"Come on, Grandpa. Let's get you back home and into bed."

"Into bed? Damn it, girl, I just got *out* of bed."

"You keep up this attitude and I'll take you over to Celeste's myself!"

"Good," he grunted. "That's what I'm hoping for."

They drove home in silence. Kat settled Homer on the couch watching a talk show then went into her bedroom to prepare it for his stay. As she changed the sheets on her bed, she let her mind wander back to the exquisite lovemaking she and Michael had shared the previous night. He was just about to tell her he loved her again when Homer broke her train of thought with a summons for something to eat. His tone was still demanding, and she wondered if Dr. Noble could prescribe him a happy pill of some kind.

"Coming, Grandpa," she called back, sighing.

She was filling a glass with ice when she heard the doorbell ring. Before she could get there, Homer was already at the door. "Hi, guys. Come on in."

Three elderly men shuffled through, and immediately they started shrugging off heavy coats, hats, and gloves. Because no one had said a word, Kat simply stood and watched.

"Did you bring the cards and poker chips like I told you, Harold?" her grandfather asked a man with a tiny mustache and a ring of white hair around the lower part of his head.

"What do you think, Homer? Have I ever let you down?"

"Yeah, that day you promised to golf with me and stood me up for that brunette with dandruff."

"That 'brunette with dandruff' happened to be my wife. Besides, that was fifty years ago and I didn't have a choice. It was my wedding day."

"Poor excuse."

Kat took the three old men's coats while wondering when this little party had been arranged.

"What have you got to munch on, Kat?" her grandfather asked.

"I'll go look," Kat said. But the four men followed her into the kitchen, sat down at the table and began dealing the cards.

"I don't have anything to drink," Katherine told them a moment later. "I'll have to run to the store."

"Beer and nuts, please," Homer requested, picking up his five cards.

She stared at him, hard. "You're really trying to take better care of yourself, aren't you?"

"Your mother holds her age very well, Homer," Harold said, and all the men chuckled.

In resignation, Kat went to the store for beer and nuts.

When she returned home, Michael's Jeep was parked at the curb. She found him in the kitchen with the older men, and the smell in the room threatened to choke off her air. All the men, including Michael, were smoking cigars.

He looked up at her with a boyish grin. He had one of Homer's baseball hats on backward, and he was holding a hand of cards. "Hi," he said, smiling.

Her mood lightened immediately. Michael looked so young and damn cute that Kat wanted to do erotic things to him right there at the kitchen table. Instead, she set down the groceries and opened the window over the sink. Opening a can of mixed nuts, she put them in a bowl and placed that on the table.

"Thanks, honey," her grandfather said. "Did you get the beer?"

"Coming right up," she replied in a sweet tone of voice. They were going to be ticked when they saw what she bought, but it was her own little way of getting even.

"Fake beer?" Homer was the first to whine. The rest quickly chimed in.

"Hey, Kid," Homer said, turning to Michael. "Why don't you run and get us some real stuff. We'll hold up the game until you get back."

"Don't even think about it," Kat said, folding her arms. "It's not even noon yet, and these gentlemen have to drive home. And Homer, you're not supposed to be drinking at all."

"Deal the cards, Louie," Homer said with resignation. "I've heard that tone of voice before from her grandmother, and I'm here to tell you we lost this battle. Let's see if we can get the Kid to part with some of the loot he's hoarding up on his mountain."

Kat stood behind Michael and watched the game for a few minutes. He held his own for several hands, but then she watched as he folded to Homer with an extremely strong hand. Resting fingers on his shoulder, she gave a little squeeze, leaned down and whispered into his ear, "How come you weren't this nice to me when we were playing *Life* the other night?"

Michael blew a smoke ring into the air before answering back. "I didn't trust your motives, but I'm over that now."

His smile was genuine, and it warmed her heart.

"You guys ready for some sandwiches?" Kat asked.

Grunts of approval surged through the smoky room.

Kat fanned the air in front of her nose. "That does it. This smoke is making me sick, and it's my house. Put 'em out now, or no food."

She started putting together sandwiches. Michael was suddenly by her side.

"Could you use some help?"

She grinned and gave him a nod.

They worked side by side, rubbing against each other every chance they got when no one was looking, and with Michael's help everyone was eating hearty submarine sandwiches in a matter of minutes. Afterward Kat cleared up the mess, and despite the protests from the other men, Michael went upstairs to work on the extra room. The old men complained they hadn't won near enough quarters from him yet, but he promised to play again another day.

Finished with the dishes, Kat left the men to their game and went to tackle a few other duties. She called her shop and checked in on Sandra; then she did a bit of bookkeeping. A short time after that she went to find Michael. He hadn't given her a good kiss for hours, and she intended on collecting.

"What do you think?" he asked as she entered. "This is the last coat of paint. Are you going to like it with the oak beams?"

Kat stood in the center of the bare room and turned. "It's perfect."

He walked over, holding his paintbrush behind his back, and leaned down to kiss her forehead. Katherine couldn't resist. She turned her face and kissed him gently on the lips. He put the brush down, and their kiss soon turned to one filled with passion, hot and lusty.

Kat unbuttoned Michael's flannel shirt and slid her hands over his belly, lightly brushing his nipples, then back to the soft hair atop his belly once more. Without losing any intensity of the kiss, Michael gently backed them up and pushed the door shut. He latched it without looking; then he lifted Kat's feet off the floor and crossed to the window seat. He sat her on the bare wood and removed his shirt, never taking his eyes from her face. A moment later the soft flannel shirt had been folded and slid under her.

Michael pressed close with a strength and power that scared Kat just a tiny bit, as did the fact that her grandfather and his friends were downstairs, but excitement ruled all. Her panties were removed in one motion, and Michael was above her once more. The winter sunshine through the window showered his naked torso with golden light.

As Michael came to her with full force, Kat held on to the loops of his jeans and gave in to her own desire, all while vaguely wondering if they could be seen through the window from its lofty perch above the street. But she need not have worried, because soon their breathing had fogged the glass completely.

# # #

That evening, Michael and Kat enjoyed dinner by candlelight with Homer and Celeste. Outside Kat's cozy home it was snowing softly again, but Kat was both content and tranquil. She had everything she wanted.

"Kat, honey?"

Homer's tone got her attention, and she looked at him with concern. He sounded serious.

"Celeste and I have decided to get married."

Tears immediately sprang to Katherine's eyes. She looked from one glowing face to the other, and any objections and concerns she might have voiced flew right out the window, including her fears about Homer dying in Celeste's passionate embrace. The pair looked as in love as she'd ever seen anyone, and after the past few days, she couldn't say there was a better way to go.

Standing, she went over to them, and with an arm around each she took the couple in a tight embrace. "I'm so happy for you. You're a very lucky man, Grandpa." She squeezed Celeste's hand. "This lady is a treasure."

"You're not tellin' me nothin' I don't already know way down to the tips of my toes."

"And you, Celeste…" Kat found that she couldn't speak. Her heart was full of love for her grandfather and the example he'd always been, and she was also flush with the happiness of her own situation. Kat flung her arms around his neck and gave him a fierce hug while announcing, "He is the absolute best."

She lost her composure, and Michael took up the slack while she tried to regain control. He leaned over the table and took Celeste's hand in his, kissed it and said, "Homer is indeed a very lucky man. I'm not sure he deserves you, but if he ever mistreats you he'll have to answer to me." Then, with a hearty handshake, he congratulated Homer. "When's the big day?"

"Two weeks from Saturday."

"What?" Kat didn't try to mask her surprise.

"I told him that was a little soon," Celeste said, shrugging her shoulders. "But you know your grandfather."

"What's there to wait for?" Homer argued. "Who knows what life has in store for a person next year—or next week, for that matter? I don't want to waste a minute of the rest of my life wondering what to do next. I just want to do it."

Kat found herself convinced.

The four of them sat around the table for another hour, each of them bringing up thoughts and ideas about the event. Kat and

Celeste made long lists of things to be purchased and taken care of, as well as beginning a guest list.

"I thought this was going to be a small event," Homer said after intense discussion on the proper flowers for a winter wedding.

"It will be, dear," Celeste assured him. "But there are certain things a wedding must have or it's simply not a wedding."

"The only things you need for sure are the bride and groom and a judge," Homer snorted. "I've heard enough. I'm going to bed."

"And I've got some friends to contact," Celeste announced. "I'll go home and make my calls, and I'll see you all tomorrow." She gave Homer a quick kiss on the cheek and left the house.

"See?" Homer sighed, staring at the door. "We're not even married yet and the honeymoon's over. I'm already playin' second fiddle to her friends. It'll be Bunco every night." He sounded sincere, but there was a twinkle in his eye that said he didn't believe it for a minute.

Michael grinned and glanced over at Kat.

"Come on, Grandpa," she said, rising to her feet. "Let me help you to the bedroom."

"For cryin' out loud, girl. Will you quit motherin' me?" Then, with a much kinder tone he added, "Goodnight, you two. Thanks for everything. I'm glad everything's back the way it should be."

Kat grinned at him and watched him shuffle off. But when she turned back to Michael, he took her hand and led her to the living room sofa. After a few engrossed kisses, Michael backed away. He looked like he dreaded what he was about to say.

"Kat...I have to go away for a couple of weeks. Actually, it's closer to three weeks."

Disappointment filled Kat's chest. "When?" she asked. "For what?"

"Later this week. I have to fly to Switzerland. I've been thinking about buying a ski resort there. The plans have been in the works for months, and I finally have investors from all over the world meeting me there. It's going to be long and involved, and I'll try to make it happen as quickly as I can but I'm not certain exactly how it will all work out."

Kat felt like a little kid who'd just been told she wasn't having Christmas this year.

Michael continued, oblivious. "After the last few days I was hoping that you could go with me, but now with the wedding coming up…well, I'm just assuming you'll want to be with Homer and Celeste. Hell, *I* want to be with Homer and Celeste. And you. But after all this work I can't cancel or postpone, and, well…"

The fact that Michael wanted her to go with him gave her strength. This wasn't just about him and his needs; he was trying to see to all his responsibilities. "I appreciate the invitation, Michael. Another time I would love to go with you, but you're right: the wedding must come first. We'll have plenty of other times to be together. And besides that, I have obligations of my own at work." She took Michael's hand in hers and raised it to her lips. "I'll miss you. I hate like hell to see you go after having you back for such a short time, but I've got lots to keep me busy until you return."

Michael nestled his face into Kat's neck and began to nibble on her ear. "Have I told you today that I love you?"

"I believe so," she whispered. "But I'd love to hear it again."

"I love you, Kat."

They spent the entire night together on the couch.

Chapter Twenty

The next two days flew by. Michael and Kat finished remodeling the extra room, and Homer's health continued to improve. Celeste and Kat started making plans in earnest for the wedding. It would be small, but maybe not as small as Homer would have chosen. Kat decided his heart could handle it.

That evening Michael invited Kat to his condo for dinner. She took an extra long time preparing for their date, as she wanted to look extra beautiful. This would be their last night before he left for Switzerland. She also drove slowly and carefully up the mountain; it had snowed most of the day and she didn't want a repeat performance of the other night. But the road to the resort had been plowed and sanded, and Kat arrived safely a few minutes before seven.

Michael, wearing a denim apron, greeted her at the door.

"Hi, you don't have to ring the doorbell. I'd like you to feel at home here," he said. He kissed her lightly on the cheek and went back into the kitchen. "Take your coat off and come and talk to me while I peel the shrimp."

"Are you serious?" Kat asked. "Are you really cooking shrimp?"

"Just one of the many things you don't know about me. I've learned how to cook a lot in the last two years. I got so sick of eating out, I had to."

"I'm impressed." She grinned at him. "I like the idea of coming home every night to a home-cooked meal."

Michael had indeed learned to cook. The shrimp, sautéed in butter and lemon pepper, were exquisite—and the steak was cooked to perfection.

"You mentioned that there are other things that have changed about you. Would you care to elaborate?" Kat asked, resting her chin on threaded fingers and smiling across the candlelit table. "Going by this, I'm kind of looking forward to learning them."

Michael stared at her so long that Kat started to feel uncomfortable. "God," he finally said, "you are so very beautiful. Do you have any idea how much I've missed that face?"

Kat shook her head. Her eyes never left his. "I feel the same way about you. Sometimes I used to lie in bed at night and try to recall your every single feature. Other nights I would have given anything to forget them."

"I know exactly what you mean." Michael shut his eyes as if trying to dispel an ugly memory. "God, the pain, Kat. I don't ever want to go through that again. We've got to take our time and make sure we're doing the right thing for both of us. We have to really trust each other—and mean it."

Kat knew he was right to be concerned, but she hated the thought of taking too much time. She wanted him in her life right now, every day and every night. She wanted to be a couple again, to live together, to get remarried and start a family. She envied Homer's fast wedding. Her impatience could harm their relationship, she knew, but she didn't want to wait. The rebuilding process had to be done together.

"How slow do you plan on taking this?" she asked.

"As long as it takes. I think we need to date each other for a while, spend lots of time together as we really are and see if that works. I think it's important to make sure we're both fully committed before we decide to get married and have a child."

"I agree," Kat told him honestly. "But I don't want to wait for a *long* time. How long do you think it will take for us to get on solid ground?"

"I can't answer that, Kat. But I feel good about us. We're going to be fine." Michael took her hand and held it across the table. "I love you. I do know that much. I just want us to make this time last forever."

Kat stood and went to his side of the table and sat down on his lap. "Me, too. I'm going to miss you for the next three weeks."

The thought of being apart seemed to overwhelm Michael as much as it did Kat, something she couldn't have imagined two years ago. He clung to her and kissed her with a fervor she hadn't known he possessed.

"Wow," she said after he seductively took two of her fingers into his mouth, sucked gently and then released them "There *are* other things I don't know about you. You're sure you haven't been practicing on someone else?"

"No," he said with a grin that melted her heart. "The opposite. I've been saving up my best stuff, and now I'm ready to transfer it to you."

"Be my guest."

Their lovemaking was tender, and oddly enough it was different than any of the other times in the past week. They were more responsive to each other's needs, though this happened almost without effort. They tried their old favorite ways of pleasing one another but also tested a few new areas of exploration; it was like they trusted each other enough to experiment. The morning light dawned before they slept.

When they woke, after a quick breakfast of coffee and bagels Kat drove Michael to Salt Lake City and the airport.

"I'll try to get finished up in Switzerland and be back in time for Homer and Celeste's wedding," Michael promised.

"I hope you can. I know they want you there," Kat said. She sighed deeply, remembering the times he'd made promises in their previous marriage. But things were different now. She loved and trusted him no matter what. They loved and trusted each other.

"I hate to see you go," she added. "I really wish I could have gone with you, but with work and the wedding, there's just no way. And it's important for you to get this done."

"Yes," he replied. "But I'm going to miss the hell out of you."

"Will you be able to call?"

"Sure. I'll call when I can. It'll be super busy, but I'll manage."

Kat waited while Michael checked himself in, and then they walked arm in arm toward the security check gate.

"When I get back, Kat, I want to concentrate on us. Let's plan on starting our life together. How does that sound to you?" Michael asked.

"Wonderful," she replied. They hugged tightly and then she said, "Please be careful. I can't stand to think of anything happening to you."

"I'll be fine," Michael assured her. He kissed her on the forehead. "We're going to be fine. I promise."

# # #

Kat got back into her old routine, at least mostly. She tried to catch up on the work she'd missed while she'd been with Michael. In the evenings she spent a lot of her time at Celeste's taking care of wedding arrangements.

Homer had moved in with his fiancée, and Kat had her house back. It felt strange coming home to its hollow emptiness after having Michael and her grandfather there, but at the same time she didn't mind being alone as much as she once had. She didn't mind her own company, and she had the promise of a future with Michael that warmed her.

Michael kept his word. On the fourth night, Kat picked up the phone and heard a slight hesitation on the line. She knew it was him before he said a word.

"Hi."

"Hi, Michael. How are you?"

"I'm okay. Missing you."

Kat let his words float over her. She shut her eyes to the ecstasy of hearing that love in his voice and said, "I miss you too, Michael."

"Is everything okay? You sound a little depressed."

"No, I'm just a little tired," she admitted. "I've been burning the candle at both ends, trying to get caught up at work and help Celeste plan. When I finally get to bed, I fall asleep instantly."

"That doesn't sound like the girl I've been dreaming about day and night. A bed is involved, but no sleeping," Michael said.

Kat smiled, imagining. "Really? Would you care to elaborate?"

"I'd love to, but I don't think phone sex is such a good idea from a million miles away. Besides"—his voice took on a low tone—"I think I'll save myself for the real thing."

"How long have you been gone, now?" she asked. "Four years?"

"Four days, my love."

"I could have sworn it was much longer."

They discussed Michael's project for a few minutes and then talked about the things Kat was handling at work. And then: "How are the wedding plans coming?"

"Just fine. They said this was going to be just a small get-together for a few friends, but it's turning into a major event. Are you going to be back in time? Do you know yet?"

"I hope so. I'm planning on it. I've had a few barriers, but I'm trying to get them solved in time." He paused, and she had the feeling someone was saying something to him. "Well, I hate to hang up, but I've got to go. I'll call in a couple of days, Kat. You take care of yourself. You mean a great deal to me. And Kat, I'm looking forward to being with you again."

"Take care, Michael."

After she hung up, Kat sat on the edge of the bed for a long time thinking of the strange twists life takes. She had bought Michael at an auction to make a baby, and now she didn't have a baby and the scheme had almost cost her everything. But she had him back in her life, and Homer and Celeste had found each other. She loved her house, her job, and most of all her ex-husband. Even if he was in Switzerland, they had a future she believed in.

Kat curled up on her bed and let her mind imagine what life would be like with Michael again. She fell asleep happy, knowing she had so many things to be thankful for.

Chapter Twenty-One

For the next ten days Kat worked hard to get ahead at the shop. She wanted to have plenty of time to spend with Michael when he returned, but to be honest the long sessions were exhausting; she kept waking up in her work clothes after having lain down in them. She spoke to Michael a few times on the phone, but the conversations were short and she missed him terribly.

A few days before the wedding, Georgi called her at the shop. "Hi, girl, are you ready for the big day? And is Homer?"

"I think so," Kat said. "I'd forgotten how much work one of these things can be. And I must be getting old. After working here all day and then helping Celeste tackle the details, I absolutely pass out at night. How are the kids?"

"Just fine."

"And Gordon?"

"Perfect." Georgi gave a contented sigh. "But listen, Kat. I've got to pick up the kids from school so let me tell you why I called. I've made up a sample of all the things Celeste wants at the wedding, and I was wondering if the two of you could drive down and make sure they're exactly right. I know the wedding cake will be okay, that's my expertise, but this catering stuff is new for me and you know how nervous I get when I cook for other people. I've also got two or three different kinds of flowers to choose for the cake."

"I'm sure we can do that," Kat assured her. "We've got to come to town tonight for the last fitting on the dress, anyway. Would seven be too late?"

"No, that would be great. I'll have everything ready. It should only take a minute."

"Georgi," Kat said, "you're a sweetie. I know Homer and Celeste appreciate you too."

"Well, you know how much I love Homer. He's been my favorite grandpa since the seventh grade when he asked my grandma if she knew the difference between sex and a ham sandwich. She said no, and he said, 'Boy, would I like to take you to lunch!'"

"Yeah," Kat said. "He's still using that."

"I'll see you at seven," Georgi said with a laugh.

That evening, Celeste and Kat talked details all the way down the canyon and into Salt Lake City. Their first stop was at the dressmaker. Celeste twirled in front of a full-length mirror in a beige chiffon gown with a beaded neckline.

"You look so beautiful," Kat said.

"It seems kind of foolish to spend so much money on a dress I'm going to wear one time, but how many times do you get married in your life—unless you're Elizabeth Taylor?"

"I'll bet you ten-to-one that Ms. Taylor got a new dress for every single one of her marriages. I don't think it's foolish at all."

Celeste turned to face her. "What are you going to wear at your wedding, dear?"

Kat was startled. "I hadn't thought about it. I don't know the timing and I'm not sure how Michael will want to…"

A raised eyebrow was Celeste's only response.

Kat tried to explain. "We're going to spend a lot of time together and take it easy. We want to make sure everything's right for both of us. We never want to make the same mistakes we did. The next time we marry, it will be for the rest of our lives."

"I think you're wise, dear," Celeste agreed. "But don't take too much time. Marriage is a commitment. Commitments don't get easier to start, they only get easier to maintain."

Kat thought about Celeste's advice on the drive to Georgi's house. Could a person take too long to be sure? Could he or she grow too independent and never want to fully commit? She loved Michael, and she wanted to need him and be needed. She liked that she'd been happy for him to go off and tackle his business in Switzerland, but she didn't want to not care that he was gone. There was a fine line between too much and too little. She just hoped that in the next few months they would be able to determine where that line was and never cross it again.

As Kat pulled into Georgi's driveway, the front door flew open and two strawberry-blond five-year-olds with bouncing curls came running to the car. "Hi, Aunt Kat! Aunt Tara's here too."

"Hi, girls. How're my two favorite twins in the whole world?" She noticed that neither of them had bothered to put on coats or shoes, so she added, "Your mom will strangle us if you catch cold. Let's get back in the house where it's warm."

The two kids each took Kat by a hand and dragged her into the house.

Tara gave Katherine a big hug and introductions were made to Celeste.

"Mom, Aunt Kat's here! Hurry!" they called.

"I'm changing Alex's diaper, Kat. I'll be right in," Georgi responded from the bedroom.

Kat introduced Celeste to the twins: "These are Georgi's girls, Kristen and Courtney."

"I'm pleased to meet both of you," the older woman said politely, bending to take the hand of one of the girls. "Are you Kristen or Courtney?"

Both girls giggled and scurried from the room, which led Kat to explain, "They never divulge that secret to anyone."

"How many children does Georgi have?"

"Three," Tara and Kat answered at the same time.

"Some days it seems like twenty-three," said Georgi as she hustled into the room. Her hair was as curly as the twins' and the very same color, and a cuddly little boy clung to her hip. She moved through the room like a tornado. No grass ever grew under her feet. "Hi, you two. Hold Alex, will you, Kat?" she asked, handing him over without waiting for an answer. "I'll get the food ready for you to sample. Why don't you come into the kitchen? Tara can you help me for a minute?"

Georgi removed a tray of hors d'oeuvres from the fridge and placed them on the counter.

"They all look scrumptious," Celeste remarked. Kat felt her stomach lurch a little. There were so many types of food all on one big platter.

"It'll look different, of course, because we'll have a silver tray for each entree, but I just wanted you to taste each one. Help yourself." Georgi stuck a toothpick in a spicy meatball and put it up to Kat's mouth. "Here, try this first."

Alex turned his head away, and at the tangy smell Kat had the urge to do the same. She opened her mouth and bit into the ground beef and onion concoction anyway…and her stomach took a nosedive. But there was nothing wrong with the food, she knew; Georgi was an excellent cook. Kat just wasn't hungry. She quickly swallowed and mumbled something about the meatball being delicious.

Georgi didn't seem to notice anything wrong. "We've got baby wieners in cocktail sauce, a peppery cheese dip, egg salad finger sandwiches, and stuffed mushrooms wrapped in a strip of bacon." She picked up a mushroom and waved it in front of Kat's nose. Kat shut her eyes against an intense wave of nausea and almost dropped poor Alex.

"Hold the baby," Kat told Tara. Choking, she spun around and raced to the bathroom. As she emptied her stomach into the toilet, Kat heard Georgi's disappointed voice float back.

"That wasn't quite the reaction I was looking for. Has she been ill?"

Celeste's voice was lower, but Kat could still hear her. "Not that I know of. She has mentioned that she's been feeling tired lately, though. And now that I think about it, she's looked a little pale."

"Yeah," Tara said. "She has."

Kat rinsed out her mouth. When she turned from the bathroom sink, the twins were standing in the doorway.

Kristen turned to Courtney. "Yuck, that's gross."

"Yeah," chimed in Courtney. "Aunt Kat's going to have a baby like mommy did."

Kat's mouth dropped open. She stared down at the two five-year-olds in sudden dawning horror.

Georgi had heard, too. "What did you say?" she asked, walking over, kneeling down and turning her daughter to face her.

"When *you* barfed like that, you had Alex."

Slowly, Georgi raised an incredulous face toward Kat. "Are you?" she asked.

Tara's mouth was hanging open. Kat didn't dare breathe. Slowly her hand moved from her side to her flat stomach.

Georgi's eyes grew rounder. "Well, are you?"

"No! I don't know. I…" Kat's voice trailed off and came back in a whisper. "I guess I could be. It's so unlikely, but…"

"Have you missed?"

"Yes, but only by a week or so. I figured it was because I've been so tired and busy."

"When you were with Michael"—Georgi had no qualms whatsoever about getting right to the heart of the matter—"I thought

225

you said he was taking precautions. You said you'd made peace with that."

Kat noticed Celeste staring curiously at her from the kitchen. "Michael?" she repeated in a stupor.

"Yeah, you know, that guy you've loved since college," piped in Tara.

"We used protection mostly."

"*Mostly?*" Georgi snorted. "It only takes once. Trust me on this. You go sit down. I'll be right back." The redhead had her coat on and keys in hand in thirty seconds or less.

"Where are you going? Kat asked.

"To buy a pregnancy test."

Chapter Twenty-Two

Kat brushed her hair and sprayed it one last time. She looked in the mirror at the lovely dress Celeste had insisted on buying for her; the pale pastel green matched the pallor of her skin perfectly.

Wedding day, she thought. And then for some unknown reason she said it aloud. "A wedding day."

But not her wedding day. It was her grandfather's, for Heaven's sake. Life was indeed strange. She was single and pregnant, and her grandfather was getting married at eighty-six years of age. She was proud that Homer and Celeste had asked if the wedding could be in her home.

No one knew about the pregnancy yet, with the exceptions of Celeste, Georgi, and the twins. Kat had insisted that her grandfather have his day in the sun before he learned, and she couldn't even comprehend the conversation she needed to have with Michael. She had spoken to him a couple of times on the phone since the night her test showed positive, but she hadn't mentioned a thing. Over the phone was not the proper way of handling this—though she'd thought it might be a good idea so that he couldn't kill her.

Kat's mind kept recalling the things they'd talked about on their last night before he went to Switzerland, about conceiving in wedlock and deciding together when the perfect time to attempt that would be. About taking their time, about knowing for sure that they were right for each other before bringing a baby into the picture. All those well-chosen, logical notions had flown right out the window. Fact: Kat was pregnant with Michael's child.

She was terrified about how Michael would react. What if he saw this as yet another reminder of her betrayal? On the other hand, she was excited. She didn't think the worst case scenario would happen. In her heart she believed their love could overcome anything, and so on the last time they'd spoken she could hardly contain herself.

She'd thought of a hundred different ways to tell him: "On the way home from the airport could you pick up some pickles and ice cream?" "Did you know that 'baby' is a four-letter word?" "Would you rather be called Father or Daddy?" "Do the words, 'the rabbit died' mean anything to you?"

She hadn't used any of them. Yesterday Michael had called to tell her, with much regret, that he wouldn't be back in time for the wedding; there had been a snag in the last of the negotiations and there was nothing he could do about it. Kat's disappointment was only temporary. Actually, it seemed to come as a blessing. She could get the wedding over with and *then* figure out the best way to tell Michael what was on the horizon.

Kat heard the doorbell ring and realized it was time for the guests to arrive. Tara and Georgi were busy in the kitchen, and she could hear their laughter; the warm atmosphere filled her with a strong sense of family. She walked into the living room and took one last look around making sure that everything was in place. She only had one more minute of peace before the house would be ablaze with friends and laughter.

"You look lovely, my dear. And the house is perfect." Homer leaned over and kissed her on the cheek. "Thanks for everything you've done for us."

She put her arms around his neck and gave him a big hug. "It's been my pleasure, Grandpa. I love you."

"And I love you. I wish the Kid could have been here, but I know it can't be helped. Are you okay with it?"

Kat nodded. "You know, it's different this time around. In the past Michael promised to be home and then called at the last minute to cancel, and I would be furious. This time, I know it's all fine. I trust him completely. I know he would be here if he could. I hear the sincerity in his voice and I believe it. Maybe it's just me. I've grown up." She sighed. "I miss him, though. At least this way he'll be home in a few days and here to stay."

She wondered where he would be sleeping when their lives resumed. They hadn't discussed if they were going to live together, or anything else for that matter. Maybe when he found out about the baby he would explode! But, no. When she really thought about it, a calmness swept her. She trusted Michael. She would soon see if he trusted her.

The minister asked everyone to take a seat. Homer, Celeste, and Kat found their places in front of the fireplace with their backs to the audience. As the ceremony began, Kat could feel her knees getting weaker by the second. She prayed to God that she wouldn't have to excuse herself to go to the restroom.

# # #

Michael's cab screeched to a halt in front of Kat's house. "Thanks, Harry," he said, handing the driver a fifty-dollar tip. "That was the scariest ride I've ever had. I'm glad I'm here in one piece."

"You said twenty-five minutes for the tip," Harry stated. Then: "Looks like they're havin' a party without you."

Michael grabbed his bags and walked around to the back of the house. He sat them down on the porch, removed his overcoat and straightened his Armani suit. Then he stood by the kitchen door and peered through its glass.

He could see Homer and Celeste through the crowd. Their heads were directed toward the clergyman before them. Kat stood to the right of Celeste. He had missed her so much, he wanted to go to her and embrace her right away. He wanted to go right up, take her in his arms and never let go. But he couldn't. Not with what he knew. He breathed twice to keep himself calm.

Adjusting his tie, Michael opened the kitchen door and stepped in. He waited for Homer's slight nod then quickly and quietly entered the living room behind the small audience. Then he walked up the aisle and slipped into his position of best man. The clergyman continued to speak of love, and of the effort it takes to make a commitment such as marriage. Michael stole a glance to see if Kat had noticed him yet. She stared straight ahead as if completely invested in the minister's words.

"Homer," the minister said suddenly, "you and your lovely lady may be seated."

Kat's grandfather wrapped Celeste's arm with his own, and the couple sat down in the two empty seats on the front row. Michael watched Kat's face change from confusion to recognition and surprise that Michael had returned and was now standing in front of her. But the next expression was joy. Pure, unadulterated joy.

She stepped into his arms and kissed him. "Michael! You made it back in time for the wedding!" She processed then that Homer and Celeste had seated themselves, and that everyone had witnessed her display of affection. Turning back to Michael, she raised a questioning eyebrow.

He addressed her formally. "Katherine Blake, I have loved you since the day I met you, through our trials and tribulations, and I love you still. The one thing that life has taught me these past two years is that we should always seek joy—and you, Kat, are my joy. Without you, my life is simply incomplete. I don't need any more time to figure that out."

She just stared at him, uncomprehending, so he gently took both of her hands in his. "Will you please, once again, be my bride? Right here, right now, in front of our friends and family?"

Katherine glanced back at the crowd, and Michael saw it just dawning on her that many of their closest friends had somehow made it on the guest list to her grandfather's wedding. Georgi winked at them both.

Kat turned back to him. "Are you telling me that this was the plan from the beginning?"

Michael nodded.

"What about Homer and Celeste?" she asked, turning to them.

"Not for us dear," Homer said loud enough for the whole room to hear. "Celeste and I are just going to shack up together. The government would nab half of our social security if we got married. This is your day, honey. You deserve some happiness."

"Yes, dear, don't worry about us. Your grandfather and I are more than happy to live in sin!" Celeste said with a wink. The audience responded with a joyful laugh.

Kat turned to Michael with a look of adoration and amazement. Then Michael watched her expression change from happiness to horror. Her face suddenly took on the same green pallor as her dress.

Georgi stood up and collected something from the kitchen. She walked to Michael and handed him the gift bag and a small velvet box, and Michael spoke quickly. "Kat, I brought you a token of our love from Switzerland. Open it now, please."

Kat took the package. Her fingers shook as she pulled the tissue from the bag and reached for the contents; then she lifted free an exquisite hand-crocheted sweater. Pure white and soft as down, it was a tiny *baby* sweater.

"You know?" she asked incredulously.

Michael could only nod. His eyes and throat were full of unshed tears.

The audience sighed. Both Georgi and Tara had tears in their eyes.

Michael held up the velvet box and opened it. An exquisite blue diamond glittered from within. "I thought this might add a bit of sparkle to that silver band I notice you still wear on that chain around your neck. So, now, my love. Will you take me as your husband and as the daddy to our baby? No more waiting. Those days are gone."

Tears streamed down Katherine's cheeks, and she shook her head up and down. She would have paid any price for this, but this was something you could never buy.

"Oh, Michael," she cried. "We will!"

About the Author

Lyn Austin is an award-winning author and a popular guest lecturer throughout the world. She travels extensively, but her favorite place is in her picturesque riverside home on the Snake River in Idaho, where she hosts retreats for writers and artists. She has interviewed over ten thousand women worldwide for her non-fiction book *Prism of Light; 22 Questions That Will Help You Discover Your Own Endless Possibilities.* However, Lyn's real passion is writing fiction. She believes that the best gift she can give the world is a couple hours of sheer enjoyment by escaping into the depths of a good book.

Readers should feel free to contact her at lyn.austin222@yahoo.com.

THE AUCTION

Every woman wants Michael Blake. Smart, handsome, sexy, he built Eagle's Nest into the hottest ski resort north of Park City, Utah. Now Michael is up for sale. In conjunction with a charity bachelor auction, he's donated a week of his time to one determined bidder.

That bidder will be Katherine Blake. Time is running out, so her plan must succeed. She doesn't require Michael rekindle the one-of-a-kind love that led to their marriage. He needn't atone for the mistakes that led to their divorce. All he need do is renovate the gingerbread home they bought together...and one other secret thing. One tiny, astoundingly beautiful yet impossibly awful thing. And with the help of her friends and her willful Grandpa Homer—if Homer will stop picking up women long enough to help—Kat is going to see her dream come true.

Did you enjoy this book? Drop us a line and say so! We love to hear from readers, and so do our authors. To connect, visit www.boroughspublishinggroup.com online, send comments directly to info@boroughspublishinggroup.com, or friend us on Facebook and Twitter. And be sure to check back regularly for contests and new releases in your favorite subgenres of romance!

Are you an aspiring writer? Check out www.boroughspublishinggroup.com/submit and see if we can help you make your dreams come true.

www.ingramcontent.com/pod-product-compliance
Lightning Source LLC
Chambersburg PA
CBHW070614130626
46556CB00001B/367